Jim Nash read order

Jim Nash The Beginning
Pirate Cay
Thrill Kill Jill
Greetings From Key West
Lost Paradise
No Angels
Mexico Gamble
No Picnic
Fallen Angels
Vendetta
A Girl's Best Friend
Dead End
No Harbor
Dog Days
Startup Blues
Last Stop To Nowhere / The Last Goodbye
Revenge Is Justice
Escape
Wedding Bell Blues
Snap Brim Fedora Caper
Breakdown
Little Girl Lost
Forget Me Not
All The Glitter
Mexico Time
Partners In Crime
Shop Till You Drop
Lobo
No Free Ride
Gone
Stealing America
Blame It on Djibouti
Trouble in Paradise

SEASONAL
Trick or Treat
Helping Santa

JIM NASH INVESTIGATES
The Snap Brim Fedora Caper
The Lady in White
The Lady in Yellow

Print Books

Jim Nash
Jim Nash The Beginning
Gun Crazy
Gun Crazy 2
Gun Crazy 3
Fallen Angels
Last Stop to Nowhere
Revenge is Justice
Escape / Forget Me Not
Wedding Bell Blues / Breakdown
Mexico Time
LOBO
No Free Ride / Gone
Stealing America
No Escape
Trouble in Paradise

Harry Delaney Adventures
Dead Reckoning
Lie Cheat Steal
Uncharted
Go-Around
Sand Storm
Harry Delaney Adventures

Frank Ross Biker Tales
No Way Out
Bad Girls
Bank Robber Dames

Other
The Last President

Check out all six books in the Harry Delaney Adventure series. Find out why Harry makes his way from the North African desert to the Mexican Baja. Discover how he ends up having a triumphal return to the deserts of North Africa.

THE LAST PRESIDENT

PX DUKE

1

It was a cold, cloudy day in January when the President-elect took the oath of office. The deluge began immediately thereafter, making the day even more dreary. The sky opened up and poured forth.

A sea of umbrellas unfurled at that very instant, not only as protection against the elements, but also as a shield against the forthcoming wave of brain-baffling bullshit. Immediately, the President declared it to be the sunniest, warmest, and largest gathering in the history of Presidential inaugurations, ever.

The campaign had been a long and difficult one. Eighteen months of politicians moving their lips. A sentient human being knew that every word passing through those lips was a lie.

Muslims.

Immigrants.

Walls.

Illegals.

Jail.

Lawsuits.

Homeless bums.

Crooks. Thieves. Liars.

Those last three very much resembled the politicians mouthing the words.

Apparently, they were all to blame for the long list of troubles now faced by the country following the election.

The president would solve it all for the good of the country.

The acceptance speech said so, with even more moving lips.

Short sentences.

Short words.

Easy to understand for even the most muddled or challenged person imaginable.

After all, the President had to appeal to his base. Had to let them know he listened. That he cared.

It was evident to many more than a few citizens that he was lying through his teeth. That he had been for eighteen months.

His lips moved again and congratulated himself on doing such a good job of winning. It was hard work, standing up in front of a bunch of fawning admirers. Convincing them the world had gone to hell in hand-baskets constructed by foreigners.

Declaring that he would do the hard work to correct it all was too easy.

All he had to do was move his lips. Short words. Short sentences. That was the key with these uninformed and confused, ignorant people.

Muslims. Immigrants. Walls. Illegals. Jail. Lawsuits. Thieves. Liars and lying liars.

It was easy as apple pie and ice cream. Mentioning hot coffee didn't hurt, either.

Nor did picking on people.

Women.
Men.
Blacks.
Whites.
Handicapped.
Challenged.
Poor.
Criminals.
The country was rigged. No one knew how bad it really was. Except the man on the podium whose lips moved, congratulating himself for the second time. And the third. And fourth.

Yes. It was a done deal. The election had been won. The best person for the job had been chosen by an electorate of poorly educated, confused, and muddled citizens. Racists. Crazy people. Ignoramuses. Bullies. Woman-haters. Pussy grabbers.

They ruled the roost now, and they knew it. They were so happy to acknowledge they now had someone just as muddled in the White House. No longer would their concerns be ignored.

A major mainstream news network conglomerate endorsed the candidate when it said he was good for the network's bottom line. How long would it be before the pundits, the other networks, the corporations, local and municipal governments, piled on? No one knew. But it was coming.

It was too easy not to.

What color would the shirts be? Brown? Blue? A red t-shirt, perhaps, to be topped with a red ball cap and a prominent four-word logo.

Overnight, the country that had been feeding the world its bullshit since the end of the last great war they helped win, was forced to eat its own shit.

Spoonful by spoonful.

The Klan.

Riots.

Muslims. Jews. Foreigners. Immigrants. Anyone speaking with an accent.

The rest of the world watched in fascination and outright horror. The country that backed dictators, thugs, middle east princes and criminals throughout the world was on the verge of doing the exact same thing to itself when the newly elected President took office.

The mess of a man standing in front of the teleprompter couldn't stick to his speech. He tried. His finger wasn't long enough to reach the prompter to follow along. He was even less able to follow along with each word. He often went off-script. He more often couldn't regain the thread of what he had been reading.

Words of single syllables worked best. It took longer than expected. He kept referring to the mess he inherited. How he would straighten it up. Fix it. Make it all great again.

A screaming man, foaming at the mouth and enraptured by the words and the proceedings, attempted to bully and kick and fight his way through the crowd of adoring fans. He fully intended to rush the pulpit. Shake the hand. Kiss the ring.

Someone screamed.

GUN!

Another screamed.

ASSASSIN!

Shocked, the crowd silenced momentarily, unbelieving, and then took up the call.

Kill him. Kill him.

Hang him.

Deport him. Throw him out. Throw him out.

Secret Service agents hustled the President off the stage. The perpetrator was marched through the crowd to an exit by private security guards hired by the President.

More unhinged screaming followed the miscreant to the door.

Punches flew. Kicks landed. Chanting grew louder.

Kill him. Kill him. Hang him. Deport him. Throw him out. Throw him out.

Wrists moved to mouths. More lips moved. Instructions were given and received in earpieces. Followed to the letter. Men rushed the President through a curtain.

Feet scrambled on concrete.

Sounds echoed off walls.

An isolated, dark hallway led to a waiting convoy of shiny, jet-black SUVs.

No time to think.

Only time to do what had been ordered.

Sudden light at the end of a dark tunnel.

Would it be the only light the nation would ever see again?

The confused President struggled to keep up with his handlers. Easy living and too much fast food caused him to huff and puff until he became completely winded.

Too many bodies comprising many pairs of hands forced him deeper and deeper into the bowels of the building.

But for those powerful arms propping him up, he would have fallen to his knees.

Holes might have ended up in the ill-fitting, five thousand dollar suit. The over-long tie might have become trapped in a closing door.

Blinding light at the end of the hallway caused eyes to blink relentlessly.

Waiting gunmen clutched at automatic rifles and pistols.

Heads turned, on the lookout for anyone or anything that might cause the operation to turn to shit.

Loud and final, a single shot exploded in the confines of the tunnel. The deafening sound compressed and echoed off the concrete walls and ceiling.

A door on a black SUV flew open.

The panicked man was thrown into the back.

He ended up on the floor in the pitch-black interior.

A crush of bodies fell on top of him, their weight forcing him even farther down.

He began to have trouble breathing with the weight of the bodies scrambling on top of him.

The announcement went over the airwaves to nearby agents. "We have secured Chicken Little. The Bucket is proceeding."

The man in the back was oblivious to the name he had been assigned.

More doors opened. Bodies disappeared inside. Doors slammed. Eager drivers raced engines on the convoy of waiting vehicles.

When it was confirmed everyone was on board, tires finally spun on wet pavement and the vehicles rushed away.

The long convoy of SUVs did its duty.

The most powerful man in the free world was rushed away from the dangers of his own acceptance celebration.

Speeding through streets.

Running red lights.

Tires squealing around corners.

Blood continued to form a puddle in the back of the President's SUV.

No one seemed to notice.

No one certainly cared.

Perhaps the gunshot had been scripted.

A cover story, maybe, in case something unexpected happened.

Someone forced a hood over the man's head.

He didn't resist.

He couldn't with the weight of the men on top of him, pretending to protect him.

He didn't panic.

This too appeared to be scripted.

Those not party to the play were behaving as they should if the president actually had been threatened.

One by one, at intervals so as not to cause alarm, wailing sirens quieted.

SUVs peeled off and separated from the long and crowded line of convoy vehicles.

Flashing blue and red lights dimmed and went out. Not so fast as to cause people to wonder. Just fast enough.

One dark-windowed SUV remained.

The lone driver steered the vehicle north, out of the capitol.

The driver kept to speed limits.

It ran no flashing lights.

It careened around no corners.

It obeyed the traffic laws as though life depended on it.

Inside, in the back, bodies finally crawled off of the

man on the floor.

The hood was removed.

A pale, white face stared back.

Eyes blinked.

Open, dead eyes adjusted.

The man was pulled upright and placed between two hulking agents.

No one checked for a pulse.

No one asked questions.

The agents stared straight ahead into the night, illuminated only by the vehicle's dash lights burning through the dark.

It was as though it was planned. Even preordained, perhaps. Part of a hoax.

Fake news.

The radio call went out.

Confirmed Clownfish is contained. I repeat. Clownfish is contained. Aquarium is proceeding as ordered.

No response came over the airwaves.

None was needed.

If you were a part of the plan, you knew it was successful.

Only the driver knew where he was to go. He had been briefed at the last possible minute. It wasn't his job to ask questions. He did his duty as prescribed by his oath of office. The vehicle he commanded carefully threaded its way through the streets and onto the northbound freeway.

An hour later, the lone vehicle turned toward the Connecticut border.

The cursor on the dashboard GPS flashed ominously, blinking at the top of the screen. The destination was near. Only minutes remained until the shore of Candlewood Lake would appear in the darkness.

The vehicle slowed and halted by an isolated, dark building with blacked-out windows.

Doors opened. Men exited the SUV.

Someone wheeled a stretcher to the vehicle. The body was manhandled onto it and covered with a dark sheet that ended up tucked neatly around the edges.

The stretcher was wheeled toward the double doors. Once inside, the sheet was removed, followed by a second hood.

The pale-faced man blinked in the floodlight-illuminated room. He squinted and blinked as his eyes adjusted. Beyond the open door, reflections gleamed off of the razor-wire, sparkling like diamonds.

The President was surrounded by men wearing bullet-proof vests. He was escorted through a phalanx of men in black, each equipped with an automatic rifle.

A pass card slipped through a lock and a door buzzed open.

A small group of men separated from the larger group and entered the room.

A single man detached himself from the larger of the two groups and removed the SUV to an underground parking area.

Lights illuminating the operation dimmed and went out suddenly, leaving the entire area in darkness. No light escaped from windows sealed against the possibility. No light entered the building from the outdoors.

A heavy steel door swung silently open on huge hinges.

The group entered and proceeded to another small area where electric carts waited. Noiselessly, the group proceeded down the incline toward another steel door. It too opened silently and the group proceeded through.

A wet stain of urine grew on the pants of the President. As a former businessman, he'd never experienced such a thing. He had remained silent for the duration of the trip, deathly afraid of forcing his kidnappers to do him harm.

Pain was not in his vocabulary or in any part of his life.

At the end of the corridor, he was yanked off the cart and directed to a room. The door slammed shut behind him and a bolt slid into place.

The President sat silent in the room, forced to listen to a set of instructions.

Videos of parts of his life that he long thought were private and forgotten flashed on multiple large monitors. The effect was hypnotizing. Visibly shaken and white-faced, he could do nothing but watch and nod his head until he was again placed on a stretcher.

Following a brief wait, a helicopter, engines idling and blades turning, prepared for takeoff. When the stretcher approached, a door opened. The stretcher was lifted aboard.

The engines came up to full power and the helicopter lifted off into the darkness. No lights were displayed.

Rotor noise dissipated into the black night. The aircraft disappeared from sight and sound over an invisible horizon.

The helicopter skimmed the nap of the earth, outbound, toward the ocean.

At one hundred miles, between Montauk Point and Block Island, it slowed and halted in a low hover.

Whitecaps appeared, stirred up by the air pulled down through the powerful rotors.

The rear door lowered and opened.

Frogmen descended into the water.

A rubber dinghy was thrown out. It inflated as it descended.

The frogmen waited.

Their patience was rewarded when a man was winched into the dinghy.

On a silent signal, the hatch closed and the helicopter climbed away. The dinghy fired up its powerful engines and proceeded east to match new coordinates programmed into the GPS.

On board the dimly-lit submarine floating just below the surface, the Admiral paced, impatient. He checked the chronograph on his wrist. Already the rendezvous was overdue.

The more time spent in American waters, the greater the chance of discovery. His eyes returned to the high-tech periscope in a vain search for the boat he knew should be approaching.

Where was it?

Why was it delayed?

How much longer would he have to wait?

The Admiral returned to pacing in the small bridge aboard the Black Hole submarine.

His orders were to wait.

Further orders were belayed until whatever was contained in the boat was secure and on board.

What could it be, he wondered?

The plans for a new missile? Perhaps even a stolen

missile.

He had no idea.

The envelope, though small, hung heavy in his jacket pocket. He took it out for another look. He handled it gingerly, as though its contents might explode in his hand.

The envelope was plain. Cream-colored and very smooth. The paper appeared to be expensive. He wondered what was so important on the boat that it required sealed orders to be opened only when the cargo was on board.

He also wondered why a navy Admiral had to be aboard one of the most advanced attack submarines in the world. He worried about passage home. The submarine would pass by eastern Canada, a country known for its ability to track submarines when they didn't want to be discovered.

He sighed and returned the envelope to his pocket. He pulled up his sleeve and impatiently checked his chronograph one more time.

It was getting very close.

The loitering submarine was sure to be noticed eventually.

How long would it be?

When would the cargo arrive?

2

Immediately after the speech, following the foiled fake attack on the newly elected President, a phalanx of supporters closed ranks to surround the stage. All access to it was blocked. If they knew what was happening, they didn't let on.

No one on the main floor heard the gunshot deep in the bowels of the building.

Reporters were unable to ask a single question of those remaining on stage. As with other such gatherings during the campaign, the journalists were crowded together in pens like pigs.

In fact, that's how they referred to the female reporters. Pigs.

They were all kept distant from the stage in wired pens.

Shouted questions went unheard, or pretended to be unheard.

Paid supporters and cheerleaders, disappointed by the early end to the spectacle, began clearing out of the partially empty stadium.

It didn't take long.

Many vacant seats spoke to the disinterest in the incoming regime.

Some dispersed to bars to continue the celebration and wonder if they'd ever get paid. Some carried on home to watch what remained of the proceedings on television.

Others, in keeping with the racist rhetoric that emerged over the duration of the campaign, searched out stores with signs in foreign languages. Small groups banded together to smash windows and doors. Random contents were heaved into the streets and set ablaze.

Firebombs were tossed into what was left of the buildings.

Shop owners were dragged into the streets and forced to watch their businesses burn.

Beatings were prolific and harsh.

Some were left for dead.

Law enforcement and police appeared to stand idly by and do nothing. Many laughed and high-fived and nodded heads in approval.

It made it appear as though law enforcement agreed with the sentiments of the rioters.

Mainstream news networks and their talking heads were flummoxed. Not one of the commentators had a clue what was happening, or what had happened. Gums flapped. They began interviewing one another. They asked themselves inane questions, over and over, looking self-important while attempting to appear to bring relevance to the hooligans.

By pre-agreement, network coverage of the riots was non-existent. Reports were whitewashed or ignored. It was determined that the dissenters were paid to provoke violence. It would make the President and his new administration look bad if burning buildings were highlighted in the aftermath of his inauguration.

Much like the political royalty, the mainstream media royalty bowed and scraped and showed subservience with gums flapping. They lied. The general populace believed them, too, thinking they had the knowledge and the access to be able to have answers for questions not yet asked.

Unfortunately for everyone, flapping gums, liars, and lying offered no solutions. Not asking questions was looking to be the new way of reporting news that didn't occur if it wasn't seen.

If there was no video, that was even better.

Fake news. It was all fake news.

Pipeline protests, occurring where they did in the middle of the nation where it was cold and windy and out of sight, didn't garner the slightest bit of attention. Military-style men, armed to the teeth and equipped with armored vehicles and dogs, used water cannons on protesters in the freezing temperatures.

For those who paid attention, such actions were reminiscent of the black protest movement of the fifties and sixties.

Dogs had been set upon them, too, by racist, bigoted state governments and their jack-booted troopers.

Fortunately for them, the local press chose to do its job. Events were transmitted live and videos ended up on television. They were played over and over again, to be viewed tens of thousands of times. Reports on the indignities committed by state employees on their citizens were transmitted to a caring nation. The governor promised Federal troops to calm a situation quickly getting out of hand.

In contrast to these modern times, no one cared.

Citizens were busy with their heads buried in their phones.

Meaningless texts flitted back and forth.

Dick pics.

Nudies.

Selfies.

Shitter texting with pants down around ankles while shit-stained fingers tapped keyboards.

Everyone believed whatever they texted was of the most importance to anyone watching and viewing.

Except.

No one read.

No one watched.

No one cared.

Intended recipients were too self-centered and self-absorbed to notice.

They were intent on broadcasting their own texts, or sending their own dick pics, or swiping left, or right, or both.

No one could see you with your pants down around your ankles while you wiped your ass and waited for confirmation.

The privacy of a restroom stall proved to be a perfect venue.

Not only were heads buried in phones.

They were stuffed so far up their own asses that it was impossible to see the light at the end of the shit tunnel that would soon be expelled like laxative-caused diarrhea.

The group was small, at first.

News spread via word-of-mouth to only trusted individuals or friends for life. Individuals from both governing houses earned membership only after being vetted by colleagues. No question went unanswered. If it did, that alone was reason to refuse entry to the entitled group.

They trusted no one. They couldn't. What they were trying to do was treason. Once the powers that be learned of their plan, it would be a firing squad. Or at the very least, imprisonment at a maximum-security facility, in a super prison.

But damn, if it worked, the world would be at their feet.

Immediately following the President's departure from the stage, a full-press court went into effect. The minions went with a story of exhaustion, as they were told to do.

What did they know? They were as clueless as the people who had cast a vote for the man.

Therefore, exhaustion following a devastatingly tiring seventeen-month campaign, didn't seem so unusual.

Except, the man had been fool enough to claim that his opponent didn't have the stamina to be the leader of the free world. So where did that claim leave him now, pray tell?

Pot, shake hands with kettle.

Except, it wasn't that man making the claim. It was his campaign staff.

The President was incapable of saying anything, imprisoned as he was deep within a nuclear bunker. How ironic, considering he once asked the question, if we have nuclear weapons, why haven't we used them?

Now would be as good a time as any.

Except, that would leave the President alive to take over.

That is not what these people wanted.

The Vice-president was next on the agenda. This was definitely a new one. Never had a Vice-president been abducted. Never one wounded or killed in an assassination attempt. It was always the president that took the brunt of those actions, Regan being the most recent. A madman who missed his mark bore the responsibility.

No, it eventually became obvious that the vice-president would have to go, too. The sooner, the better, to make sure the entire plan was believable.

Only then would the Speaker of the House be in a position to take over.

Aboard the Black Hole submarine, the impatient admiral checked his watch one more time. He raised the periscope. A boiling white wake revealed itself behind a fast-approaching dinghy. He lowered the scope and gave orders for a slow surface. The huge submarine barely made a whisper as it broached the surface, rising gently into the cool night air.

Two seamen rushed up the conning tower, pressed buttons and turned wheels. The heavy, water-tight door flipped open. Four men armed with automatic rifles followed behind. The dinghy's double engines reduced throttle and eased up to bump against the submarine.

A single man in a jump-suit abandoned the dinghy and boarded the submarine.

He was first to descend the conn.

Armed crew members escorted the man to the commander. The visitor was hustled to the admiral's private cabin by armed men.

Orders were given not to disturb.

The remaining men secured watertight doors.

The conn was abandoned.

Men returned to the bowels of the submarine to resume normal duties.

With the cargo secured, the submarine slowly slipped below the surface in minutes. It didn't make a sound. No waves. No splashing water. Nothing gave it away.

The Russian Black Hole made record time to its destination.

At a submerged speed of 25 knots, it rendezvoused with the destroyer in the Atlantic in twelve hours. In two hours, business completed, its back-course took it to the initial point of rendezvous.

The cargo was off-loaded quickly into the same rubber dinghy.

3

The announcement came a day later, on television and in newspapers. A press officer stepped into the briefing room's bright lights. The President was fine. He had been whisked away to a bunker for his own safety and security. Medical tests had been completed. His fitness for the job was deemed acceptable.

The press officer continued.

Nothing untoward had happened. The individual responsible for the fracas in front of the stage had been arrested and was awaiting a hearing by a judge. Nothing was known about him at this time. Nothing would be released by the authorities until such time as it was deemed appropriate.

Much fawning adoration had followed the President-elect wherever he traveled on the campaign trail. Crowds yelled and screamed approval. Media conducted excruciating, fawning interviews. Questions of substance were never asked. Even if they were, answers were avoided. The subject was changed immediately.

As such, following the President's swearing in, journalists continued with their smiling, respectful, lapdog attitudes. They were told in no uncertain terms that if they disobeyed their corporate masters and disrespected the President, they would end up in a bread line.

Following the fake news reports of the assassination attempt, bands of hooligans roamed streets with spray cans, painting slogans in support of the President on walls and windows and doors. Others tipped headstones in cemeteries. More broke down doors in the dark of night and set fire to shops once they had stolen everything they wanted.

Red-shirts, they were called. A red t-shirt and a red ball cap with white lettering proclaimed their allegiance to a country that would be made whole again by a single person. They had all voted for him. Why would he forsake them?

He wouldn't.

He would end up turning "his" country into his own personal shithole.

In the night hours before the President-elect was sworn in, before he took office, Russia advanced, unopposed, into Eastern Europe. Nations toppled like dominoes. The advance was reminiscent of a German blitzkrieg during World War II, minus the gunpowder and explosions.

Former member-states of the old communist Russia were overrun in a single day. Fearing retaliation if they did not proclaim appeasement, parliaments and congresses met in the wee hours of the morning to pledge allegiance to this new European world order dictated by Russia.

Then the roundups began.

Press.

Television.

Internet.

Phones.

All were shut down.

No one and nothing was omitted.

Doors were broken down.

Reporters were loaded into vans and buses and trucks.

Overnight, prisons and jails began filling beyond capacity.

In day two of the new American administration, Russian troops advanced up to the border with Germany. The country appealed to Great Britain for assistance.

Britain declined, having only just voted to pull out of the European Union via its BREXIT voter turnout.

During an emergency sitting, an overwhelming majority of British parliamentarians voted against sending troops to Europe. They would not be aiding or abetting World War III. They were an island nation, and an island nation they would remain.

Mainland Europe was a boat ride away, and not Britain's problem.

America, as a member of the North Atlantic Treaty Organization, refused to assist its NATO alliance members.

Desperate, German troops made multiple unsuccessful attacks on sites they knew to contain tactical nuclear weapons under the control of the United States.

Russia rode roughshod over all of Europe in days, thanks to American and British acquiescence.

Britain was now nothing more than an isolated island but for a small ocean and a tunnel to France. Brits destroyed the tunnel, thus completing their self-imposed exile and isolation. They could do nothing about the watery channel separating them from France.

In any event, Russia considered England to be irrelevant.

As did America.

Britain had been unwilling to honor or commit its military resources to Western Europe via NATO, of which it, too, was a member.

How could anyone not think the country was irrelevant?

America willingly relinquished its domination over the European continent.

It agreed to pull all of its troops and military equipment from its bases in Europe.

Russia consented to wait until America completed its evacuation of men and nuclear weapons. Once they received the signal, the Soviet Union would position itself to occupy what little remained of Europe.

By the third day, Russian warships and submarines stood off the coasts, unchallenged, to set up a defensive perimeter.

American warships and transport aircraft were allowed free access during the evacuation process. All others were shot down or were forced to land in the new Soviet Territory.

It was as though it had all been pre-arranged and pre-programmed.

The Chinese Dragon watched what was happening with a certain intense jealousy. Not to be outdone, and sensing an opportunity, it was convinced that the American paper tiger would do nothing.

China advanced on southeast Asia.

Naval blockades were set in motion.

Southeast Asia fared no better than the European Union.

Yet again, America refused to intervene.

Australia attempted to stand up to the dragon. Although it fought bravely, its navy was destroyed in the process.

An appeal to the United States for assistance under the ANZUS Treaty was denied, citing a phone call between Australia and the United States where the Australian Prime Minister reportedly hung up on the American president.

American media deemed the Chinese attack to be fake news. The media ignored any and all reports from their own military.

Wanting to keep its aircraft intact for the defense of their continent, Australia brought everything it had remaining home.

The Chinese man-made islands in the sea did their due, acting as the extended boundary for the country. Hong Kong, Malaysia, all of them, were overrun by the Chinese Dragon.

The more far-flung island countries were put under naval blockade en masse by Chinese forces.

There were skirmishes in Europe and Southeast Asia. How could there not be? Most were small, and the participants were rogue members of various military units from some of the countries that had been invaded and overrun.

All were resolved quickly by overpowering military force.

In Europe, revolutionary groups quickly grew in

France and Germany, financed by Saudi oil sheiks. One such group managed to obtain two tactical nuclear weapons.

Berlin was sacrificed by the freedom fighters for what was believed to be the better good. In retaliation, Hamburg and Munich were destroyed by the Russian invaders a day later.

Paris was sacrificed following the detonation of the second stolen nuclear weapon.

Marseille and Toulouse were nuked hours later. In many parts of the world, it was believed that to take retaliation so quickly, it all had to be part of a plan.

It was not long after that continent-to-continent communications were severed. Internet, telephone, landline, telegraph, radio signals, all went silent.

Each and every nation found itself isolated.

In a week, thanks to a massive military and civilian airline operation, America had its troops home.

Massive unemployment dominated the economy.

Banks and other financial institutions failed.

People were left homeless by the millions.

All forms of government assistance ended abruptly.

Unable to obtain foreign financing for its expenditures, the federal government was humbled. All of its programs were broken and broke.

Individual states fared no better. Deprived of federal funding for many programs, they raised taxes overnight on individuals to abhorrent levels. The intent was to fund everything from infrastructure improvements, sports arenas, and their own lifestyles.

Corporations and the wealthy paid extremely low to no taxes. The reasoning went that without them, no one would have a job.

Millions demonstrated in favor. Most were unemployed or unemployable, thanks to an education system that no longer worked for anyone.

With an upside-down economy, high unemployment, and a lack of jobs for the returning troops, America entered a downward spiral.

Bread lines were fake.

Reports of rioting were deemed fake news.

It was proclaimed that paid dissenters caused all the troubles.

Time after time, the President took to the airwaves and the twitter twits declaring everything to be improving. The economy. Jobs. Infrastructure improvements. Everything was booming. The size of government had been reduced substantially to ensure the military had appropriate funding.

Taxes went ever higher.

Medicare and Medicaid benefits were slashed or cut altogether.

Social security was cut and finally eliminated.

Senior citizens lost all of their benefits, including the ever-popular and extremely useful Wheels for Meals. Such programs were deemed unproductive and incapable of achieving results.

It was only a few months before needy senior citizens were being hauled from their apartments, homes, and boarding houses, as they became unable to pay for housing.

Public transport was eliminated.

Infrastructure spending declined to nothing.

Minus funding, failing sewer and water systems

became contaminated.

Cities began falling apart.

Trash was dumped in the streets.

Rats ran rampant.

Police departments faced massive budget cuts.

The law and order the President had promised failed to materialize.

A previously successful program offering health care to one and all was outright canceled. Overnight, the death rate increased, no thanks to death panels, but more from a lack of doctors. Hospitals and pharmacies cut back services drastically. There was no longer anyone able to afford to pay.

What was left of the broken banking industry went into receivership and received bankruptcy protection. Anyone left with a bank account was forced to pay an annual fee of 10 percent on each of their accounts just for the privilege of keeping their money on deposit. Consequently, many withdrew everything and stashed it in their homes and apartments and cars and back yards.

Thefts and robberies went through the roof.

Underfunded police departments were unable to respond. Rather, police management concentrated on increasing the numbers of drug arrests. Property confiscated as part of the process of crime increased. Unfortunately, because no one was making a meaningful living, police auctions went unattended, leaving them stuck with properties that went without maintenance.

Basically, everything went to hell in a hand-basket. No one was unaffected.

Except for the military.

The money saved by cutting programs for the poor, small business, schools, health care, the elimination of

Medicaid and Medicare, all went to the military to fund manpower and equipment that would never win another war.

Not to worry, though. Reporting on the problems faced by the country was classified as fake news.

In contrast, the President declared everything rosy. Lying liars in the media were making the problems up to discredit the government's success.

Promises were made to lock them up.

Thunderous applause and cheers went up on hearing the words.

Pep rallies. That's what they called them. If you didn't go, your neighbors tattled. Vans showed up. People were hauled off. No one knew where. No one asked questions.

They were too scared.

Eventually, neighbors stopped wondering and learned that not tattling was bad. Tattling was good. Six words became the mantra.

If you see something, say something.

Neighborhood spies took to reporting everyone and everything to certain authorities deemed necessary for the good of the country.

Lies were told.

Falsehoods emphasized.

Ever more people were rounded up.

4

Russell

No one ever noticed I was a spy. Perhaps it was because I was so good at it. Or just maybe it was because there was no one left to notice.

See something, say something, indeed.

I liked to sit in an easy-chair at a corner of the large, south-facing window in the front of the house. I would crack the bottom corner of the curtain just a bit and look out over the small expanse of neighborhood before me.

I enjoyed observing the sun on its early morning climb. It would bring light into the dark corners of the yards in the cul-de-sac fronting my new home.

Sometimes, in the evening before sundown, I would do the same. I'd take up the chair and wait for the sun to set. For the daylight to darken. For the neighborhood to go black. When it was over, I would let the curtain drop to its rightful place.

I don't know why I bothered keeping watch. Perhaps it was from some perverse sense of responsibility, knowing I was the only one left to guard the knowledge of what had happened.

Or perhaps I hoped beyond hope that one day, I'd look out and there would be someone in my world just like me.

Open and welcoming as I thought I would be to the prospect of another human being entering the world I inhabited, there was still the chance that whoever showed up might not be in the same frame of mind.

So I took precautions.

Under no circumstance did I want even a single ray of light to make its way past the blackout curtains at night. No part of the night needed to be illuminated. I couldn't have anyone walking up to a window wondering why there was a stray ray of light escaping the house. It became part of my routine to go to each window nightly, checking and re-checking the curtains for leaks.

Before settling in to my new house, I went around the cul-de-sac and pulled the curtains in almost all the abandoned homes. I wanted every house to look normal from the outside. I wanted everything to look normal. I had to convince myself that there was nothing that appeared abnormal about my neighborhood surroundings.

Only then would I permit myself to fire up the generator.

It gave me light. I had heat. I had food storage. I had hot and cold running water.

As long as I felt safe in my neighborhood, I didn't care about anything or anyone else. I didn't care if I ever saw another human being again.

Lie though that was, I truly might not have cared, but for the loneliness.

I'm not sure when the craziness began in earnest. I'm not even sure what started it.

Perhaps it was a Presidential election that returned a child-like, incompetent man as leader.

When I still had friends who hadn't gone into hiding or disappeared, we would steal time together to watch an old movie called Being There. It was about a person who had learned all he knew about the world from watching television.

That pretty much nailed it for me.

It didn't appear to be good for the country, however. Some suspected some sort of a deal had been arranged. By the time ordinary citizens woke up, pulled their noses out of their phones, and began paying attention, it was too late. There were too few of us remaining.

Foreign powers had neutered all of Europe and the Far East. Consequently, communications had been shut down between countries and continents.

No one could find out for certain what was happening in the world. There was no way to find out beyond what little local media and the odd radio station reported. And all of that was government-sponsored.

Propaganda, most likely. Or maybe it was all truly fake news. No one could tell for certain any more. All the mainstream media had sold out long ago.

The best I could come up with on my own concerning the fiasco was inconclusive.

A report got out that meteor showers would occur over a couple of days. What media there was encouraged everyone to get outside and have a look at the spectacle as it unfolded. Plainly visible through night and day, the exploding bright flashes were accompanied by smoky, dusty trails extending behind for miles.

Much of the television and radio coverage at the beginning of the two-day extravaganza turned into rabid fever when experts couldn't, didn't, or wouldn't explain why the meteor showers continued for two weeks past the forecast end date.

That the broadcasters then turned to amateurs espousing all sorts of religious hokum and fakery came as no surprise. After all, the quacks and shysters made for colorful visuals and exciting sound bites.

Not a one of them, be they expert, quack, or bible-thumper, had any reasonable or believable explanation for why the sky had been turned into a never-ending light show that had gone on for weeks on end. What had been billed as a one-time explosion of meteoroids suitable for viewing by both adult and child alike turned into a side-show event.

Only the ticket booths were missing.

At the end of it all, a fresh batch of authorized news and television reports were pushed out by bored commentators when the six-tailed asteroid was discovered. In keeping with initial reports of a two-day meteor shower that lasted for thirty, none of the supposed experts the government called on knew anything about six-tailed asteroids.

A spectacle such as that was brand-new to them, too.

At least the asteroids could only be witnessed by those designated to peer through huge telescopes squatting atop mountain observatories. Every once in a while, television news would coax some university egghead to venture forth from his hole, like the fabled, eager groundhog anxious to see if the sun might be shining.

The poor soul would position himself in front of a bookshelf, hoping to look erudite and impressive, and fumble with a mess of papers scattered randomly across a monstrous desk occupying most of his office. Mumbled, incomprehensible jargon would follow.

No one could understand a word the purported scientist said.

When the interview concluded, a network team of reporters would make an attempt at repeating and interpreting what had been said. Ignorant as the rest of us, the media ass-hats made even less sense than the egghead. Instead, they preened in their three-thousand-dollar suits and began interviewing each other.

None of it made for good television.

The egghead who caused it all ended up scurrying back to academe, never to be heard from again.

Radio broadcasts fared no better. None were capable of describing or painting an oral picture of the chaos. There was no one to interview that could make sense of what was happening. Charlatans and fools ended up being commissioned to do the bulk of the radio spots. Eventually, television caught on and moved to use the same uninformed experts to turn the sky's unfolding events into religious and voodoo scams and shams.

The final insult to anyone with a modicum of intelligence occurred when someone randomly mentioned the sun's magnetic poles were about to reverse. Never mind that this happens every ten to twelve years. Radio and television evangelists ran with it as another sign of the pending apocalypse.

The hoarding began slowly, just as it had under other false religious prophets in other years and decades. At first, it was only a trickle, and went unnoticed. It wasn't long before the trickle became a flood, and everyone began trying to catch up to everyone else.

It seemed as though anyone who was capable of thinking for themselves became a risk to others.

If you didn't jump on the prophecy bandwagon, you had to be silenced.

Toward the end of the third month, news reports of measles outbreaks in South America and to the north in Canada began circulating. That, coupled with reports of the deadly Ebola virus growing out of control in West Africa, pretty much guaranteed that panic, enforced by the authorized Western news media's fevered reporting, would ensue.

Whether it was more fake news couldn't be determined. It was too late for that.

It wasn't long before street-corner encounters started. The gatherings began with a small-town atmosphere in the rural outback of the state. Then cities large and small caught on to the idea. Four and five people to begin with, growing by dozens and then hundreds as word of the rallies got out, ensured that the wave would be impossible to stop.

Distrust of the media grew daily. Fake news reports proliferated. Alternatives were put forward. Most of those were believed.

Many, if not all, of the gatherings were encouraged and pushed by religious zealots and fundamentalists in churches and basements, in the past infamous only for their predictions of world disaster and catastrophes that never occurred.

People who wanted to believe in the end times

listened anew.

The same tired explanations came straight out of bible scripture, interpreted and preached with a religious zealotry unknown in the past.

It wasn't obvious at first. Then, stores couldn't keep their shelves filled. They began to run out of everything. First water. Then canned goods. Flour. Rice.

It all disappeared, slowly at first.

Then faster and faster.

Eventually, it became too late to halt the panic, particularly when media caught wind of it and started their version of panic in the streets. Despair was fueled by hourly updates and breaking news headlines plastered across television screens.

First, it was the more populous states that called out the National Guard. States with smaller, more isolated populations were the last to call out the Guard.

By then, it was too late.

No one knew it at the time.

5

I **wasn't the first** to make the connection, nor would I be the last. I had been a little slow on the uptake, though. When I finally pulled my head out and looked around, I realized trouble was definitely afoot. I was pretty sure I wasn't alone with that diagnosis, but since I just moved to the city, I didn't have friends to confer with or to ask for advice.

I was hoping the move would do me good. I wanted out of the prepper rut everyone I knew was joining.

I would have moved back to where I came from, but by then it was impossible. Commercial flights were closed but for inbound international flights. All forms of ground transport had been eliminated. It had become impossible to go or to move anywhere, ever since local and state governments had coordinated and declared their states of emergency.

Last to that waltz were the feds.

It made for good television, and that meeting of the so-called minds was broadcast live.

I sat, transfixed, watching the mindless politicians listen to the military chiefs-of-staffs explain what needed to be done.

When it was over, martial law had been declared. All roads and interstates had been shut down. Travel was restricted or outright forbidden.

Six months in, no one was permitted to go anywhere, not even to visit dying relatives.

Airports were next. Air travel anywhere was terminated. Domestic air travel was limited to flights within each state. All small, private aircraft were grounded. Attempts were made by some to commandeer private aircraft, although it was never determined where these people would go. Every airport in the country was closed to all but government air traffic.

Agents were dispatched to local airports and flying schools to gather up the names and addresses of pilots.

That made for good television, too. News conglomerates friendly to the government's talking points—which pretty much meant all of them—were embedded and dispatched to film the raids during which the miscreants were rounded up.

SWAT teams descended in haste from black vans. Residences were surrounded. Doors broken down. Pets that made a sound were shot. Entire families were loaded into vans and hauled away, in plain view, day and night.

No one seemed to know where the people were being taken.

No one seemed to care.

By then, television and radio spots on home-built radio stations were being broadcast twenty-four hours a day. Stay inside. Don't go out after dark. If you're caught, you will be shot on sight.

Even the mobile stations weren't safe. Many of them appeared and disappeared overnight.

Grocery stores turned into relief centers. One family member was allowed to collect a daily ration, no more than that. If the line was too long and you weren't able to get to the front by hook or by crook, too bad. You turned around and went home empty-handed.

All this while walking or riding a bicycle. Because by then, there was no gasoline. What there was had to be reserved for official business—and that was more like official funny business. More commonly known as monkey-business.

At first, those same relief centers were good for catching up on rumors and gossip. It was presented as fact that certain parts of the city were first to be emptied. No one knew why, or how, or where the people had been relocated or shipped.

Early on, I made the decision to move from my walk-up apartment near the city center to the now empty outskirts. I told myself these areas had been abandoned. I knew differently. It wasn't so.

Getting there involved dodging stalled cars and trucks and piles of empty pallets and tins. Some of the major routes had been cleared by heavy equipment. Abandoned vehicles had been pushed off the roads. They ended up on sidewalks or in ditches like so many toys.

Only the major routes were treated that way. It had to be to facilitate the occasional military convoys I crossed paths with. It was more difficult to avoid the stench of garbage stacked on lawns or left piled in the streets.

In my travels, I had acquired a battery-powered bicycle. I scrounged two solar panels to sling on either side of the rear wheel, and a third to strap to my backpack. My biggest problem was keeping the bike from being stolen when I went to pick up my ration.

I solved that one by moving again into one the hundreds of houses close-by that had been deserted and left empty. By then, the owners had been run off, or, more likely, rounded up and shipped to the camps or wherever the powers that be were shipping people.

When the dwindling population dictated that the ration centers close, I began a search for a new place. I found one a lot farther out in the burbs.

The isolation suited me. Surprised by that, I made my fourth and final move even farther out into deserted suburbia.

So far, I had been lucky. I managed to avoid being spotted and picked up during the daily sweeps performed by National Guard troops. The huge, loud diesel patrol trucks were easy to avoid when they made the only noise around for blocks and blocks. The sound of their coming gave me plenty of time to get the bike into a back yard, out of sight of anyone but the most nosy neighbors.

There weren't many left to be nosy.

Nine months into the purge, there appeared to be no neighbors. No one. Nothing. I had given up on ever coming across another human being. I was beginning to feel like a rat abandoned in a maze of my own choosing.

And I was still lonely.

I vowed to move—move number five—one final time.

It felt like forever before I located my current home, but it took only a week. For seven days, I tramped through neighborhoods from sunup to sundown.

I dodged patrols.

Hid out in dumpsters.

Climbed onto roofs to get my bearings.

When I lost my place on the paper maps, I used the sun to get me back to someplace familiar where I began all over again.

I opened doors.

Inspected.

Followed stairs down to basements.

When at last I found a house with a built-in water reservoir, I made my decision in an instant. The collectors and piping directed rainwater into below-ground storage tanks. That the tanks were indoors made it even more secure.

It would take time to turn the place into something I could use to survive.

I scoured abandoned hardware stores for electrical wiring, outlets, switches, tubing—anything that could be used to hard-wire a gasoline generator.

In two days, I had the generator working, muffled and safely exhausted into the back yard through a window in a spare bedroom.

The generator had enough juice to run a fridge and a small stove and a microwave on a part-time basis.

I even found a small instant hot water heater that ran on 110 volts. I loaded up with extras for spares.

It took another day to run wiring from a small fuse panel into the kitchen and the bathroom.

I installed the heaters into the house's existing water lines beneath sinks. Each heater in turn could be shut down. I didn't need them all working at the same time.

It took time to make my new home secure and livable. To guarantee electricity, I had to stock up on gasoline. Fifty-five-gallon drums and a hand pump would do for that. The drums I rolled into the garage, empty.

There was plenty of gasoline remaining in abandoned automobiles. To collect it, I used smaller containers that I hauled in a wagon behind my bicycle. A small electric pump with an intake line that could be fed into gas tanks allowed me to suck each of them dry.

I took simple pleasure in the task of setting the clock on the microwave each time I powered it up.

Eventually, I got over that.

I never got over the loneliness. Or the silence.

The blackout curtains hanging over all the windows pretty much guaranteed that.

I was comfortable in my new surroundings. Comfortable and safe. I knew from my daily patrols and excursions in search of consumables to stockpile that there was no one left.

I was on my own, safe in the knowledge that no one would disturb my life of quiet solitude.

Even so, there were still occasional patrols to avoid.

6

The **day began like** any another. The sun came up as it always did—not that I was expecting it to do anything else. The beginnings of its enlightening orange glow began its revealing rise over what I considered to be my small neighborhood.

The day's scavenging would be done beneath a bright blue sky.

I made sure to slowly lift a corner of the curtain a mere couple of inches. I needed a good look before I exited my house. Satisfied, I went to the front door. Just to be sure, I flipped aside the cover over the peephole. With a single eye pressed to the narrow opening, I cast an outward glance.

Shocked, I pulled back and ran to the front room. I raised a corner of the blackout curtain covering the huge window. Someone striding purposefully across the cul-de-sac's short street disappeared behind a garage.

In a state of panic, I almost yelled and rapped on the window. How dare that person invade what I considered to be my space, my property? Shaking uncontrollably, I sank into the chair in front of the window reserved for spying.

The man's shoulders had been hunched beneath an oversize hoodie. It hid his head and guarded his face. A baseball cap pulled low and dark glasses obscured the face from the front.

In the time it took to collect my wits, whoever it was passed by, unknown and ignorant of my presence.

That was all right by me.

I dropped the corner of the curtain like a pot too hot to hold. I felt like a home-owner who spotted a dog crapping on his lawn while the owner of the dog did nothing to prevent it.

The sight of another human being put the fear of being discovered into me.

I barely remembered to check the time. The diary entry I made in my normally steady hand was shaky and hard to make out. I moved back to the window and lifted the curtain, perhaps expecting to find some remnant of the visitor's presence in my cul-de-sac.

Now I knew for certain what I had always suspected.

There were others.

How could I have thought I was the only one? I resolved to remain at home, indoors, and await the trespasser's return. Surely he had to retrace his steps on the way home.

How long had he been out there? How long had he been traipsing through my neighborhood? Who was he? Where did he live? Was he only one, or were there others? A small group, perhaps, banded together for protection.

My mind raced. It would cost me a day. Maybe even two or three. Perhaps more. I had to know. I resolved to remain indoors for the entire day to see if he backtracked through my cul-de-sac on his way home.

Excited by the prospect, yet fearful, too, I couldn't stop pacing. Prior to this, I had no idea. I encountered no one on my travels other than the random, roaming military patrols. They were obvious testament to the thoroughness of the evacuation plan. Or the purge, if that was in fact what it was.

A purge. No way could I comprehend. I'd given up trying.

I brought my lunch from the kitchen into the living room in preparation for the all-day vigil.

It didn't take long.

My hidden observation post and the diary I kept provided me with a sense of how often the transgressor passed through my neighborhood. Whoever it was, they were doing recons for their own purposes, just as I had been doing.

Twice a week, regular as clockwork on Monday and Thursday, early in the a.m., the person would pass by. Usually he would retrace his steps by mid to late afternoon. The pack he carried, empty in the morning, would be full and heavy on his back by afternoon. He too was stocking up with whatever he could find.

Being the resourceful type, I resorted to binoculars and studied the walker up close and personal. That's when I recognized the walker for what she was. My curiosity piqued, I began to pay even more attention. A creature of habit, the woman's schedule took her through my neighborhood on a regular basis.

The double-barreled shotgun was sawed off. She wore in a sling across her front. That alone gave me pause.

How could I not have noticed it before? Was I fortunate not to have encountered her while we were both out scrounging? Certainly, the shotgun gave me worry. How amenable would she be to crossing paths with another human being?

Not very, judging by the firearm and the bandolier of shotgun shells she chose to wear.

With time to kill and not much else to do, I waited her out. More often than not, and usually like clockwork on those two days, I'd be rewarded. She would trudge past early in the day, backpack empty. By day's end, she would labor past on the return trip.

Judging by her slow, measured gait, the backpack had to be extremely heavy.

By now, the woman had filled the viewfinder in my binoculars so many times I could judge her age. She had to be in her mid-twenties, perhaps a bit more. Long—haired, perhaps. I couldn't tell for certain. Her hair looked to be in a severe bun when she wasn't wearing the hoodie or the ball cap.

Hippy-looking, the way she dressed, but like me, she would have been too young to know much about that generation.

She always wore a long-sleeved shirt and long pants and hiking boots. A bandana covered her neck against the sun when the hoodie got left behind on those days when it was too hot and humid.

She was doing exactly what I was doing, and doing it quite well, judging by the way she carried herself with the full pack. She had to be in good shape.

I wasn't brave enough to follow her. I considered it. Then I thought it best to leave her alone for the time being. I didn't want to make it look like I was some sort of stalker bent on taking everything she had for my own.

Besides, she had that shotgun. She could end up with everything I owned and then some.

That alone was worrying. I hadn't thought to collect any weapons. Since spotting her, I became more nervous each day I went without. To put quiet my nerves, I considered getting my own weapon. Perhaps I was naive, to say the least. There was probably more like her around, even if I hadn't yet caught sight of them.

Over time, I made sure the loneliness of my existence had become bearable. To do it, I had kept busy. Now, since catching sight of this woman, I realized how lonely I really was all these months.

I began thinking again about a partner, someone to share this new world in which I found myself trapped. I returned to my own search and acquire missions.

I had to. Winter would be on its way soon enough.

I spent too many sleepless nights thinking about the woman trespassing on what I considered my private property. My personal cul-de-sac. Who was she? Where was she living? Were there others? Were there others partnered with her?

My waking hours weren't much different. On those days when I knew she wouldn't be passing by I returned to my own scavenger hunting. It was only on my breaks, when I wasn't occupied with keeping out of sight of marauding National Guard patrols, that thoughts of the woman intruded.

Even then, it was only more unanswered questions that came up.

My map got a workout in a futile attempt to estimate how distant she might be. If she behaved anything like I did, she would be up at first light and out the door shortly after to get a good start on the day. Still, it was a lot of ground to cover, and it could be anywhere, north, south, east or west.

Eventually I'd have to follow her to find out. That I knew for certain. I didn't look forward to it, considering she was armed. That sawed-off shotgun across her chest was more than enough to force me to keep my distance in person, if not in mind.

I felt even more alone now I knew I could have had some company in my lonely life. I spent a lot of time fantasizing about the woman, wondering what she was like. If she'd be friendly toward me. Whether she might consider me an enemy, someone in competition for the resources we searched for on a daily basis.

I began to look forward to seeing her on those days when she passed by. If she missed a day, or sometimes two, I became despondent, worrying about her well-being. Had she harmed herself? Tripped and broken an ankle or a leg while hoisting the heavy pack? Perhaps she'd given up and moved on to new, unexplored areas.

Then she'd return, and I would almost jump for joy. The first time, I did. When I spotted her, I did an embarrassing happy dance behind the curtain.

She was back. She was all right. She was safe.

7

Caitrin

Caitrin considered herself lucky to have a job. Graduating as a communications major with a minor in psychology hadn't presented many opportunities.

The small, on-line company that sold doomsday prep gear took a chance on her. She intended to prove them right about providing her the opportunity. Green as she was, when necessary, she applied what she had learned as best she could. She worked hard, learned the lingo as she went along, and ended up pleasing the business owner with her enthusiasm.

Consequently, when the company did its monthly tests of the gear it sold, she was invited to go along on the camp-outs in the hill country to the north of the city. City girl that she was, she quickly adapted to the rigors of the overnight routine. She grew to enjoy the camaraderie of the small group of employees as well as the wilderness experience itself.

What she learned amazed her each time the group did

an overnight or a long weekend. Getting comfortable using the gear. Setting up camp. Lighting fires. Cooking. Learning survival techniques. Bugging out when the camp-outs ended. It eventually became routine for her. She was always a little sorry to return to the confines of the city.

As a result of the camp-outs, she had gotten to know one of her workmates. Soon after returning to the city from one of their excursions, she began dating Konnor.

Konnor had been raised in the city, too. He attended a small community college and studied web design. In the small company they worked for, he slowly worked his way to finally becoming a trusted employee. He stayed flexible and did what was asked of him by his employer.

Shortly after the troubles began, for that's what Konnor called them, he asked her to move in with him. She agreed. It seemed like the thing to do. Safety in numbers, even though their number was only two, appeared to be reasonable. After all, at the time, no one knew how long the troubles would last.

And, as she learned from working for the doomsday prep company, after watching their videos, after spending time at the camp-outs, she knew two people in an emergency could do twice as much as one in the sense that the work could be split and parceled out. The business owner once lectured all of them on the benefits.

The interior of the city wasn't an ideal place for either of them, but when the store and warehouse closed its doors, the owner tossed them the keys and told them to help themselves. They moved into the basement. It wasn't an ideal setup, but the concealed rooms served their purpose and prevented them from being discovered when the roundups began.

Neither of them anticipated that. Not even in their wildest nightmares, and they had never shared a bad nightmare, so far.

When the city emptied itself of every last human being, it was Caitrin's idea to get them out of the dark basement and moved into an empty house miles away in the suburbs. It took both of them three days to transport every last thing they could think of to the house. It was a job, even using two bicycles.

Occasionally, they had to take steps to avoid a patrol. The diesel trucks huffed and puffed their way around the city, but the noise the huge military vehicles created made it easy to stay out of their way. As the months passed, the patrols occurred less and less. It was as though every last vestige of humanity had been uprooted and sent packing.

To where, they didn't know.

Nor did they want to.

Caitrin missed her family, such as it had been. In truth, she missed her father. He had written off her mother when she wouldn't stop drinking. When she was twelve or thirteen, she overheard the ultimatum he gave to her mother. As with all of them before, it too went ignored. A few months after that, he packed up and left, leaving Caitrin alone with her alcoholic mother.

Her father maintained sporadic contact for a while, until she received a notice that he had passed away. When her mother died shortly after, Caitrin was the only person at her funeral.

That was probably a part of the reason she so quickly moved in with Konnor. She knew she didn't want to be alone any longer, especially given what was happening all around her.

So far, Caitrin had been happy in her partnership with Konnor. Like any beginning relationship, there were bumps in the road, but overall, it seemed to her it had been a good arrangement for both of them. They quickly moved into the traditional male-female roles of provider and housekeeper. She didn't mind, given the circumstances, even though she knew she was more than capable of helping with the providing.

When Konnor finally realized he needed help, he asked, and she threw herself into the task to the best of her abilities. She felt he had to know that as she depended on him, Konnor could depend on her.

Many days they came home exhausted from their efforts to obtain food, water and everything else they needed to survive. They would fall into bed together, too tired to make love, and too tired even for shared conversation about the day's events.

The strict daily routines they forced upon themselves sapped all of their energies. Often they would end up in each other's arms, sobbing themselves to sleep.

There was no relief in sight.

The purges, the troubles, and finally the searches to survive became difficult for both of them. Forgetfulness, bad hygiene, suspicion, depression, all vied to take over their lives.

At first, it appeared normal to Caitrin. She too was guilty of those same emotions and errors in judgment.

Konnor in particular became more withdrawn. He talked of getting out of the city. Caitrin agreed, and pushed for a move farther into the suburbs, distant from the city center. It made sense to her. It also made sense that such a move would be good for Konnor, too. She believed it would help to take his mind off of whatever was eating away at him.

The planning and the gathering of the supplies for such a move took all their time. They hauled it all into the former store that had become their residence. Then began the exhausting work of moving it to the new home they had chosen, far from downtown.

It was the firearms that finally convinced Caitrin that things were getting serious. Konnor had them stacked in a corner, complete with ammunition boxes. She didn't want anything to do with them, but he finally convinced her otherwise.

She picked out a double-barreled shotgun that caught her fancy. The ease with which she accepted the inevitable surprised her at the time.

It wasn't long before she began carrying it everywhere she journeyed in the abandoned city. She added an ammo belt strung over shoulder to the opposite waist. She began to feel more and more like a soldier of fortune, but she knew better than to believe it. She had never pulled a trigger on a firearm of any kind.

She thought the reason the double-barreled shotgun stood out for her was because she had seen them in movies. That, and it looked simple to operate. Two shells in, close the breach, pull the triggers. She would give herself bonus points if she was ever called upon to use it.

Double bonus if she hit close to what she might aim at.

Following a few practice rounds that would have woken the dead were there any within earshot, she knew she couldn't miss at close range with lead shot. When she got home that day, she used a hacksaw to shorten the barrels. A file quickly took off the rough edges.

It seemed to improve the balance, both hers, and the

shotgun's. The elimination of the long barrel made it much easier to handle when it was strapped to her front.

After practicing with it indoors, the increased maneuverability impressed her so much, she went out and fired a few rounds. Her efforts paid off. Immediately she was convinced she hadn't made a mistake.

She knew that as long as she pulled the stock tight against her shoulder and leaned into it, she'd be able to hit whatever she crossed paths with. As long at it was in front of her.

And as long as she paid attention and noticed.

Initially, Caitrin believed that the stress and fatigue from the search for a new place and their subsequent move that took forever was beginning to affect Konnor's judgment. She allowed him to sleep late and stay home for a couple of days while she carried on with the move.

It didn't improve his outlook or his attitude.

He remained aloof and withdrawn, incapable of expressing emotion. He stopped doing what they both did when they became frustrated. He could no longer laugh with her. He became unable to concentrate and couldn't remember even the simplest things she asked him to do. Eventually, she couldn't get him out of bed, no matter what she tried.

She made one last try by resorting to cooking breakfast, naked, in front of the stove.

It was hopeless. Caitrin couldn't ignore any longer what had been staring her in the face. When she finally recognized Konnor's symptoms for what they were, she panicked. Even though he hadn't been delusional or hallucinating, she knew from her psychology courses that

Konnor was becoming schizophrenic.

Further, she knew she had no treatment for him.

She began growing concerned for her future. Without Konnor, she would have been much worse off, and she knew it. He had contributed so much to her survival and her emotional well-being. Now all that was threatening to unravel because she could do nothing for him.

With winter coming on, she didn't think she could survive on her own.

Caitrin didn't want to contemplate what it would be like living with a crazy person. That was especially so when the craziness already in their lives was almost more than they could handle as a team.

If he was going around the bend, she'd have to deal with it.

If only she knew how.

8

It took Caitrin the better part of a week, but she finally convinced Konnor she should be allowed to make the daily excursions into the city by herself. She teased. She cajoled. She begged. He relented, finally, by allowing her to start with two days a week, on Monday and Thursday.

She already knew it would take months at that rate to gather up the remaining items they would need. Even so, he almost ended up refusing to let her do it at all.

She began getting up first thing in the morning. She wanted to avoid Konnor and his irrational fear at having her leave him alone in the house. She'd fix a quick bite to eat for both of them, leave Konnor's on the table, and then she went to dress for the day.

Caitrin hid the fact she was a woman behind bulky clothes. Her jeans were loose. She tucked the cuffs into the expensive hiking boots she had obtained during a smash-and-grab at an outdoor store's window display.

She considered strapping down her breasts and decided against it. A sports bra would have to do. Overtop of that went a t-shirt and a regular shirt. She added an oversize hoodie. Beneath that, a ball cap covered the long hair she kept in a bun whenever she went outside.

She checked herself in the mirror each time before she left, as if she might have missed something.

She never did.

On her way out the door, she added the shotgun and the ammo belt. From the belt on her jeans she hung a small k-bar with a handle just big enough to fit her hand.

As hard as it had been for Caitrin to convince Konnor to let her go, he never seemed to notice her disappearance on those twice-weekly excursions. Perhaps it was because she slipped out the door. She stopped saying goodbye for fear it would set him off on one of the ever-increasing rants he was beginning to subject her to.

She couldn't take the yelling and screaming. All she wanted to do when he started in on her was to escape to the isolation of the outside world.

After a while, she enjoyed the silence and the solitude more than being at home.

As the treks took her farther afield, she would often be gone all day, almost into darkness. She wouldn't allow herself to be out in the night. At the end of the day, often as late as twilight, she'd arrive home, exhausted, feet sore and back aching from the weight of the enormous pack she toted.

She knew she was using those two days as an escape from her developing problems with Konnor. She spent the time thinking, and she didn't like the one question she kept asking herself. What was she going to do without Konnor to help her exist within the confines of the deserted city?

Despite her worries, she continued to enjoy being out of Konnor's way. She got to examine parts of the city she barely knew existed. She was most cheerful when she passed through the city's parks with their huge shade trees and picnic tables. Some of them even had barbecues. It reminded her of what was missing, but she soon chased those thoughts out of her head.

She couldn't allow herself the luxury of halting the day's exercise for a barbecued steak and a baked potato, even if her mouth began to water at the thought. She had far too much to do.

Caitrin used a city map to mark out the areas she already explored. She made notes of where she might return where the pickings turned out to be good. On foot, it was slow going.

She'd tried using a bicycle, but ditched that idea when the heavy pack she carried got the better of her. She had tipped over, and in her clumsiness, knocked herself out when she crashed to the ground, driven there by the off-center weight of the pack.

Hell, even a kid knows how to ride a bike.

The shotgun didn't provide much of a cushion.

When she came to, she looked around, embarrassed that anyone might have seen her. Then she remembered she was all alone. She laughed at her clumsiness, but she walked home rubbing both her head and her ass. For good measure, she added her bruised ego into the mix.

Later, looking herself over, naked, in the mirror, she traced the outline of the huge bruise where the shotgun dug into her rib cage.

Konnor's condition worsened, and Caitrin dreaded coming home at all. She never knew what mood he would be in. She knew she was becoming the sole provider when she realized that Konnor had stopped going anywhere. More and more, his paranoia was inserting itself into their relationship and turning it into a nightmare for both of them.

She was beginning to wonder if remaining with Konnor was the thing to do. The realization that she would have to do something, and soon, about her living arrangement was beginning to dawn.

What that would be, she had no idea.

It was a shortcut Caitrin took on the two days she went out into the world. At first, it was only an eerie feeling that overtook her when she passed through one of her regular neighborhoods on her scavenger hunts. It wasn't the entire neighborhood, but only one small part.

She couldn't explain the feeling. As the days and weeks passed and she became more self-assured, she decided that someone had to be watching her. She had nothing to go by. She had never crossed paths with another soul. So why was she so insistent that someone else was there, spying on her?

The feeling was so insistent that it forced her to begin paying more attention to her surroundings. She realized she could no longer strut carelessly through the streets and neighborhoods as she had in the past. If there was someone out there, she needed to know about it.

Her senses went on full alert and she halted at the edge of the cul-de-sac. Nothing looked out of the ordinary. In fact, it looked like every other street she traversed. Almost. Something wasn't quite right about this one, though.

Her mind was already made up about it.

She thought she might start avoiding the area and

then thought better of it. If she was going to become paranoid now, in a city that she was certain was pretty much deserted, she might as well throw in the towel, stay home, and join Konnor in his crazy fantasies.

She couldn't allow herself to do that.

Then it struck her.

She stopped. She looked around.

Overhead, the sun was in just the right position to shine through the front windows of all the homes in the cul-de-sac. She examined each of them from where she stood.

Nothing looked to be out of the ordinary. However, at second glance, in what seemed to be a random pattern, the curtains in some houses were closed. In others, they were open. If memory served her right, in almost every other neighborhood she traveled through, the curtains on almost all the houses had been left open. People wanted to be witness to the proceedings going on in their neighborhoods.

With curtains closed, they couldn't do that.

It was a small thing, she knew. And maybe she was joining Konnor in his madness. But she didn't think so.

Caitrin shook her head, unable to believe what she allowed to creep into her mind. She resolved to shut it out. At the same time, she lost her concentration. She took a step and her foot slipped off the curb. Unbalanced by the heavy load in the huge backpack, she tripped, stumbled and the off-balanced weight sent her careening onto a lawn.

On her way down, a corner of a curtain moved. Or did it? She thought it did. Did it really? She couldn't be sure.

Shock moved through her body and she stiffened. She stayed on the ground, stunned, unable to move a muscle.

It wasn't from the weight of the heavy pack on top of her. She lay where she fell and tried not to move.

She could barely draw a breath.

She wanted to turn her head toward the window, but she couldn't. The huge weight of the pack prevented her from getting up. She untangled her arms from the straps. As she did, she pushed the pack away and stood up.

She couldn't force herself to move beyond that.

Don't look, don't look, don't look.

Caitrin made a show of preparing herself for an attempt to pick up the heavy pack. She adjusted the shotgun across her chest. She took her time positioning over the pack. Finally, she knelt and shoved her arms through the straps. She tottered forward and used her legs to lift the full weight off the ground.

It was all she could do to stand up.

In doing so, she rotated her body to permit her to look in the window's direction. She wasn't obvious about it. She pretended to concentrate on the pack. But she managed a quick look.

She almost went down to the ground a second time.

Caitrin couldn't allow herself to give any sign. She had no idea what she was into. First instinct after picking up the heavy pack was to drop it instantly and flee as fast as she could. She might have, too, if her knees weren't trembling so badly she could barely walk with the heavy weight.

For a split second, she again contemplated dumping the pack and taking off.

Her breathing quickened into a pant. Nervous sweat ran down her back. She couldn't drop the pack and take off as fast as her feet would let her. She wanted to. Every fiber in her body called out for her to run.

She made the decision in an instant. That she didn't run was a tribute to her resolve.

She forced herself to put one foot in front of the other and walk out of the cul-de-sac and away from the house. What she had seen had already burned itself into her brain.

Don't turn around. Don't look back. Keep moving. Keep moving forward.

There'd be plenty of time to look back if—or when—she returned.

She thought about what she'd seen all the way home. That someone else was left in the city came as a shock, although it probably shouldn't have. She'd been naïve to think she and Konnor could be the only ones who chose to hide out and remain behind.

During the long, exhausting walk home, Caitrin considered her options.

A third person would mean an opportunity to come together with her and with Konnor to help keep them all alive. That is, if Konnor didn't go completely over the deep end. She would have to take time to better assess his condition. Even as she considered that, she knew she would have problems.

Finally, she had to admit what she had been afraid of doing all along. She would have to ditch Konnor, one way or the other.

When, not if, it came to a choice of sharing a place with a madman, or one who was an unknown, she thought she should be able to make the decision easily. After all, she was a woman. And women, these days at least, had to be in short supply.

When the time came, she told herself, she'd do what she had to do to survive.

Her decision for preservation made, she twisted the key to unlock the door. Happy to be home and eager to greet Konnor, she rushed to tell him what she saw.

Caitrin heard the screaming even before she opened the door. She changed her mind and tried to set the pack down just as Konnor yanked the door open. He greeted her with a brutal punch to the face. It knocked her backwards down the steps. The heavy pack kept her on the ground. Konnor landed on top of her and kept punching.

She couldn't get her arms out of the straps. She couldn't block Konnor's fists. They rained down on her. With arms trapped, unable to defend herself, she had to take the beating. Thanks only to Konnor's extreme condition, he soon exhausted himself and rolled away.

Caitrin's brain went into overdrive. In an instant, she decided to desert the home she had grown accustomed to. The home she considered her own since moving in. This would be the last night she would spend in it.

She would have to leave Konnor behind.

As comfortable as it was, as much as she knew the neighborhood, as bad as she wanted to remain with Konnor, she knew it was over. Her life was worth more than a few possessions and a completely insane man who might end up killing her.

That night, she locked herself alone in the bedroom. Konnor pounded on the door, screaming, kicking, trying to get in. She forced herself to ignore the crazy man he had become. Still, she couldn't sleep. When Konnor finally quieted from exhaustion, she remained awake, continuing to evaluate what she had seen earlier in the day.

Who was it? More importantly, was it a man or a woman? If it was a woman, how would she get her attention and draw her out of the house?

She knew what she had to do would be dangerous. She knew too that she had to get as far away from Konnor as she could for her own safety. What she wasn't so sure of was whether it would be any safer with the person that had been spying on her walks through the neighborhood.

Toward dawn she fell into a sweaty, nervous sleep, thinking about how she would make her move.

9

Russell

In the beginning, when people were still concentrating on meteorites and six-tailed comets and the sun's reversing poles, the general roundups began. Everyone with a circular vaccination scar got ordered into refugee centers. The story publicized was that an epidemic had begun on the South American continent and it was progressing north at an alarming rate.

At least, that's what the broadcasts repeated. Some began murmuring something about fake news reports. Fundamentalists picked up the cry, reminding everyone there had never been a smallpox scare. That the scar had to be related to the mark of the beast.

I had never heard of a circular scar. I looked it up, and learned it was a mark, all right. Left by a scab. Before about 1972 or 1974, everyone had to be inoculated against something called smallpox. The resulting scab would give the recipient of the vaccine a small, circular scar for life along with lifetime immunity to the disease.

Apparently, smallpox had been eradicated from the

face of the earth sometime in the 1980s—or so the articles said. All the smallpox cultures were to have been destroyed. And also apparent, judging by the disease's advance northwards from South America, it hadn't been.

So much for trusting governments to do the right thing. Or perhaps the proponents of fake news were right.

We'd already had something not quite similar occur just before the meteors. It was called measles, and anyone who hadn't been vaccinated against it could catch it and die. Many did, for it spread rapidly among the religious freaks and anti-vax nutbars who had allowed themselves to be talked out of permitting their children to get any immunization shots at all.

When the deaths began, it seemed to me to be only right. Those who didn't see the value in modern medicine were designed to die for their supposed sins.

We all ended up paying our dues, one way or another.

Following the measles epidemic, the government began scouring medical records for the names of people who hadn't had any immunization injections. By then the black vans had been replaced by city buses painted in dark colors with yellow markings to highlight them.

When that started, something told me it was time to move, and I did, a number of times. I picked up, packed up and moved out to the burbs. I wasn't nervous or concerned about it in the slightest.

I accomplished my many moves in the wee hours of the mornings, in complete darkness, on a battery-powered bicycle. It took many trips until, finally, I was settled and alone.

Alone, that is, until I saw her again.

I checked my watch. It was time. I raised a corner of the curtain out of the way. Nothing. Impatient, I pulled it back farther and almost pasted my face to the glass. The glass fogged. I rubbed it away. If anyone was looking in, I was pretty sure I resembled a madman looking out.

Reflex action forced my head back so fast I almost tipped the chair. The woman appeared in the center of the circular cul-de-sac. With hands on her hips, she looked to be checking the houses, one by one.

I straightened and peered out again. She had to be looking right at me. I felt exposed. Vulnerable. How could she not see me? Should I let go of the curtain? Should I ignore what I had just seen? Do I keep looking out?

My eyes focused on the shotgun. The action was closed. All the other times, it had been open, ready, waiting for the shells to be inserted. It was obvious she was on guard, too.

So she had seen me that first time. I suspected as much, yet I was fearful to admit it. Now she was back to check. If she wasn't blind, she had to have seen me for sure this time.

Panicked, I ran to the door. I slipped the cover and looked out the peephole. She was on the edge of the distorted, narrow field of view. She was just getting up off the ground. She must have stumbled. Perhaps from the shock of confirming something where only moments before there had been nothing.

I rushed back to the window. I yanked the curtain wide. I pasted a grin on my face and waved. The girl halted mid-step. Both feet touched the ground. She turned on a dime and ran off in the direction from which she came.

My disappointment was complete. There was no

sense in encouraging anyone to come calling. I pulled the drapes shut. In the safety of the darkened room, I took my time to evaluate what I had witnessed.

This time, I managed to get a good look. She was definitely attractive. That's not what I noticed first, though. First was the weapon. The shotgun, the same one I'd seen her carrying. The double barrels had been shortened. A cut-off, to make it easier to handle.

The gun was slung across her front. The double-barreled breach was closed. The bandolier over her shoulder carried enough shells to make it look like she belonged to a small band of mercenaries.

If that was in fact the case, I wanted her on my side.

I tried to get her out of my mind. I forced myself to concentrate on the map in front of me.

My map was my record of everything. It told me where I had gone to scrounge for things I needed— mostly canned goods. Gasoline not so much, since abandoned vehicles were everywhere.

It was color-coded block-by-block as a reminder of where I had been. Where nothing of value remained. Where I might want to go for a look-see at what was left.

To keep a step ahead, I marked the urban pockets of farm animals that people in the city had started to collect and feed before the purge. In time, I thought I might be able to gather some of them and move them to an empty arena, or perhaps a small, fenced park where there would be grass.

Perhaps I'd get a small farm going for fresh eggs and goat's milk—all in good time.

And then thoughts of the woman banished everything from my mind. Not thinking about her would not be so easy. I realized the value of having another pair of hands and legs to help accomplish the grunt work.

Having someone to talk to and share the loneliness wouldn't be so bad, either.

It wasn't so much of a struggle any longer. It became routine. Over time, I got accustomed to the absence of people and vehicles and the silence that went along with it.

When the power grid shut down, I was prepared. Plenty of warning came as outages and fluctuating supply. Brownouts and blackouts became the norm.

In advance, I located a generator and plenty of power cables, plugs, jacks and conduit. I stored it all in the basement. Once I set my mind to it, it took only a day of dedicated effort to restore power to the house.

It seemed to me that any improvements in my situation often would lead to more work. Gasoline became my next project. I managed to collect an empty 45-gallon drum. Over time, I managed to fill it and I was good with electricity for a month if I rationed. I'd need more in the long term. I'd need an easier way to get it out of the vehicle fuel tanks, too.

Time wouldn't be an obstacle. It was all I had going for me.

It took another four months of roaming the city for me to realize just about every last soul had been shipped off to somewhere. I stopped looking for anyone to ask where they thought that somewhere might be.

There was those two times, though. That woman. She caught me looking at her through my curtained window. I let go of the curtain too late. She had to have seen the covering fall back.

I tried reversing our positions. That was when I realized when I opened the curtain wide, I might as well have been exposing myself as a naked man might. That alone would have scared me to death, too, were I on the outside looking in.

Several days passed since the second sighting. Given how I'd scared her off, I didn't think I would ever see her again.

I was in the kitchen, going about my normal routine. Homemade bread went into the toaster. Two eggs ended up in the fry pan. I sliced half of a fresh-grown tomato. The smells were killing me and I was thinking how nice it would be to wake up one morning and—

Plink. Plink.

What the hell?

Stones. Bouncing off glass. Someone was throwing rocks.

I ran to the door and put an eye to the peephole. Instantly, I moved to the window and pulled the curtains wide. I made sure to paste the same silly grin on my face as I had the other day. I didn't have to try hard. It came naturally.

She made it obvious she was looking for me. I had to wonder, though. The action on the shotgun strung across her chest was still closed. My mind raced. It had to be loaded. Two shells. Buckshot, maybe. Or slugs. Didn't matter. Either would be fatal.

When she knew she had my attention, she turned and walked away. I was devastated.

That was the last straw.

I loaded a plate and took it with a small table to the center of the cul-de-sac. I went back for knife and fork and a chair. A folded cloth napkin made for the finishing touch. If she was watching—

I went inside, closed the door behind me with good slam, and locked it. In the kitchen I started on breakfast number two. Damned if I was going to go hungry on account of her.

Disappointed and filled with despair, I ate quickly. Seeing her with that shogun convinced me I'd need weapons of my own. I checked the doors and the garage. Everything was secure. I knew she'd be watching, waiting. She would want to check the place out when I wasn't here.

That was fine by me. Perhaps it would encourage her to do more than that.

Before I headed off, I peered out through the window. On the table, something white flashed. I opened the door and checked my surroundings. Went to the table, all the while looking around. Picked up the folded note resting beneath the plate.

Thank you! The tomato was so good. I like my eggs scrambled. C.

I looked around. Was C, whoever she was, lingering? I carefully folded the note and tucked it into my pocket. I hauled everything inside before departing on my mission. By end of day I would have my own shotgun.

It took longer than I wanted. Most of the gun shops were looted of anything useful. Late in the day I ended up with a pair of shotguns. One was an automatic with a magazine. The other was a pump action.

I was only knowledgeable enough about firearms to make sure they were the same caliber. Kicking though the rubble, I discovered a book on how to modify them. I came up with a couple of bandoliers, too. The shotgun shells fit perfectly.

By the time I had the trailer loaded with ammo boxes of shot and slugs I was sweating like a pig. I threw my soaked shirt on the trailer and headed for home. By the time I arrived and stowed everything in the garage, I was physically and mentally exhausted.

I collapsed on my bed and slept the night away.

The next day's assignment took me to a hardware store. I picked up a vice and a hacksaw and blades. Some files, too. Once home, I read about shortening barrels and went to work with a vengeance. I attached slings and adjusted them across my chest. Hell, I even practiced positioning the short-barreled pump action in front of me in case I ever needed to use it.

I hoped I would never have to—probably because I knew I couldn't.

Eventually, the woman stopped tracking through my neighborhood. I almost forgot about her. Then I would take out the note I kept in a pocket and wonder about C.

Who was she? Was she nearby? Did she have someone waiting for her when she crossed the threshold of her own home, anxious for her return? Or was she alone, wandering solo around the city like me? When I ran out of questions, I was left with only a woman's careful script.

Perhaps bacon and eggs over were no longer her thing. I should have scrambled them. I gave up and stopped wasting my food.

For some unknown reason, the note always ended up tucked away for safekeeping. If nothing else, it was a part of a happy memory.

It was after one of my more successful scrounging expeditions. I turned into my cul-de-sac and braked to a sudden halt. I almost dropped the bike. The woman was sitting on my front step. It was too late to pretend to ignore her and turn around.

I pulled into the drive and leaned the bike on its stand.

"You'll get a ticket for not wearing a helmet." She smiled.

I tried not to. I wasn't successful. "Not likely. Anyone with a government gas ration and any smarts is long gone from this place. That's why I'm here."

"So then, you're saying you're not so smart?"

"I'm saying I'm about as smart as you are for being somewhere near here, too. I'm Russell."

"Pleased to meet you."

She never told me her name. I stuck out my hand. She formed a fist and instead, bumped mine. In only a split second she withdrew her hand. There was no chance to make a grab for it, even if I wanted to. I didn't try to hide my surprise. A look of disappointment washed over my face.

"I'm sorry, but I have to be careful. I don't know you," she said.

"That's all right. Give me a couple of minutes to haul everything inside and I'll make us some tea."

The woman sat cross-legged on the lawn, well away from the open garage door. Her sunglasses hung on her neck. She took care to watch my every movement as I unloaded my treasures and hauled them into the garage.

"What did you manage to collect?" she asked.

It was my turn to be guarded. "Oh, the usual. Just some stuff I think I'll need."

She took her cap off and grinned up at me with wide-open eyes. "Who's being careful now?"

She held out her hand and I helped her up.

The roaring diesel engine noise reverberated off the walls of the empty neighborhood and echoed into the cul-de-sac. By the time I recognized the sound for what it was, it was almost too late. I scrambled to push my bike into the garage and let the door down without banging.

Only just in time did I make it inside the house. In my haste, I forgot all about the woman. The huge truck rounded the corner. It halted in a cloud of black diesel exhaust and squealing brakes at the entrance to the circle of houses.

All of a sudden the location I had chosen because of its isolation had been breached in a most uncomfortable way. Even so, isolated from the outside by curtains covering windows and doors, I still believed there was no way I would be discovered.

In the darkened room, someone tapped me on the shoulder. I gasped and almost jumped out of my skin. My forgotten company just made herself known. Where else could the woman have gone on such short notice?

"Damn, woman, I've been alone in here too long for that."

"I'm sorry. I wanted to remind you I was here, too. My name is Caitrin."

Caitrin's backpack sat on the floor in the living room. She kept the shotgun in plain view. A huge k-bar hung off her belt. It was tied to her thigh. The handle had been ground down and would probably just fit her smaller hand. Then she wrapped her hand around it, and I knew

I was right about that.

I tried to lighten the atmosphere by moving to the door. I peered out the peep-hole. A single unarmed soldier descended from the truck and consulted a map. He looked down the deserted cul-de-sac and shook his head. As a last resort he climbed up on the roof and looked around.

He must have been satisfied by what he saw. He descended and drove off in a noisy cloud of black soot.

I waited until the truck moved off. I cracked the door to listen to the engine sounds becoming ever more faint. I opened the door wide to let in some light. Exhaust fumes drifted into the house.

Caitrin stirred and took up a chair in a corner of the living room. She'd be able to keep a wary eye on me.

"You look like you belong there," I told her.

She ignored the comment.

"It's going to be dark soon. I'll fire up the generator and make you some of that tea I promised before we were so rudely interrupted."

She jumped up, as though preparing to run out the door. "You've got electricity?" She was almost too excited for the words that came tumbling out.

"Yes I do. Running water, too. Whoever owned this place had the presence of mind to put a reservoir in the back yard to collect rainwater. That's one of the reasons I moved into this house," I said.

"Can I take a shower? I've been bathing in dirty swimming pools and I've about had enough chlorine to last forever."

That would be fine with me. "Towels are in the hall closet. Take a chair with you to prop against the door."

"Thank you. I will." Caitrin gathered up everything

she owned and took it with her into the bathroom. I couldn't blame her. I would have too, were I in the same position. When the water stopped running, a familiar, high-pitched whine made its way down the hall to the kitchen.

She must have found a hair dryer.

10

Russell and Caitrin

While Caitrin dried her hair in the bathroom, I considered what happened during the truck's brief appearance. I wanted to run it by her to get another person's opinion, now that there was another person.

"It's amazing what electricity, a little fresh water and a hair dryer will do for a woman. I was considering cutting my hair short before this." She halted at the entrance to the kitchen. "Oh. What—"

"Sit down. Eat. I made your favorite."

She obviously didn't want to appear ungrateful. I watched her throw caution to the wind as she took me up on the offer of food. She settled in at the table and began devouring the scrambled eggs and toast. I was left to wonder about what she said about cutting her hair. Did it mean she would return?

I left her alone to finish. When she did, dishes rattled in the sink and the water turned on. With the dishes done, she joined me in the living room, where I was studying a map.

I hoped I wasn't making it too obvious I was checking her out. She left her hat off, and her hair shone after the shower. She was pretty good looking—especially now that she wasn't carting the shotgun around inside the house.

I tried not to stare too long. I couldn't help it. She was one good-looking woman. Hell, she didn't even have the shotgun close by, so I felt brave. "Come back and shower any time you like," I told her.

And there it was. I had just made an offer. Would she? Could she? Was there someone else?

"Is that my cue to be leaving? I haven't had tea yet," she said.

How could I have forgotten?

"No, not at all. Give me a minute. I'll be right back."

She followed and stood at my side, watching as I filled the kettle. "Come on, I want to show you something."

Ever cautious, she allowed me to lead her to the back of the house where I had the generator under its sound proof cover. I showed her how to start it and to verify the exhaust vented properly outside. I told her about the blackout curtains and explained why they should be kept closed.

"If I'm not here, that's all you'll need to know to get another shower. Just don't forget to leave anything outside. I wouldn't want someone showing up and learning about my haven."

"You're right, you know. It is a haven of sorts. At least, for me it is," she said. Her gaze intensified.

Why was this woman looking at me like this? Was she sizing me up? If so, for what? I would need to be careful with this one. In the kitchen, I poured hot water into two mugs. "It should be ready in a couple. In the meantime, there are some things we need to talk about."

I tried to include the woman as best I could. I valued her opinions. After all, she'd been on her own long enough to get a pretty good idea of what had been going on, too.

"Did you notice anything unusual about that truck?" I asked. "Anything that stood out from previous trucks and their contents?"

"Yes. I've seen them before, but not like that. A single occupant, the driver. Oh, and he was unarmed when he got out."

"You have a keen eye. It occurred to me he was careless because he knew there was no one to threaten him. I'm thinking every last soul has been evacuated into relief centers."

"Or worse," she said.

I ignored Caitrin's comment. I wasn't comfortable even considering it. It might be selfish, but I had more pressing matters to consider.

An extra person to help with some projects I had planned would be nice. Until now, I never considered having a helper. It might end up doing us both good. I eased into the subject, hoping I wouldn't be obvious. "Would you like to see my workshop?"

I was constructing a solar and battery powered pump. It would provide the gasoline for the generator. The only way to get more would be to scrounge from the thousands of abandoned vehicles littering the streets and their gas tanks.

Already I had a makeshift trailer built for the bike to cart the system. Empty twenty-gallon containers sat beside the pump and the solar panels in the garage.

She took in my efforts. "You've been busy."

"When you feel more comfortable being around me, I'd like to have your help. What do you think?"

Caitrin stepped back and studied me, hands on hips, brow furrowed. "So it's a mule you need, do you?"

I refused to avert my gaze, even if she had me figured. "No, I can do it all myself. But now that we've been formally introduced, I think it would be good for both of us."

"How so?" she asked. She waited to hear what I had to say.

"You've been scouting out your own resources. I'm not looking to steal your secrets. I could use a little help with my own. That generator alone will gobble up a lot of fuel when the nights get longer and colder."

"Thus the portable pump," she said. "I can understand that."

"I've got a chain saw, too. I'll have to feed that stove when the weather turns."

I had replaced the fireplace with a modernized version of the old Franklin stove. I fed the stovepipe into the fireplace chimney. It might not be the best, but it was better than the actual fireplace.

Caitrin gestured in the direction of the park behind the house. It seemed she knew the area, too. "You don't have far to go for firewood."

"I can't start cutting down the trees in this neighborhood. That would draw too much attention the next time a lost truck driver climbs out and starts looking around," I explained.

Caitrin walked to the door. Before opening it, she looked through the peep-hole. "It's too late for me to get home. I won't have enough daylight. I don't want to be out in the dark."

I considered her words, but it was true. It was getting dark, fast. And she was probably right not to want to travel alone at night.

"You can stay here. You'll be safe."

Satisfied, she picked up her belt with the k-bar and strapped it on. "You're right. I will be."

She didn't want any of the spare rooms. I left a blanket and a pillow on the sofa.

"As for the help you want, we'll go fifty-fifty on it. After you're finished, you can start helping me with a few things."

I wasn't expecting that so soon. I was thinking she'd need more time to sleep on it.

"Thank you. It's a deal. I accept," I said.

She stuck out her hand, and this time she shook mine. It was unexpected. I walked down the narrow hallway to my bedroom. She could sleep anywhere she darn well pleased. I considered, and then I propped a chair against my door.

Secure and happy knowing I'd have company to look forward to in the morning, I slept easily. That the company was a woman, and an attractive, useful one at that, was a bonus.

Her grip was firm. Her hand was soft. That was a bonus, too.

It turned into a toss-up whether I dreamed I could smell coffee or bacon. The hum in the same dream turned out to be the generator at the end of the hall. It was then that I remembered I had company. Caitrin must have fired it up for another shower.

I threw on a t-shirt and a pair of jeans and ventured out, eager to know what I'd find in the kitchen. I was unprepared for a woman in a short, brightly colored sun dress standing barefoot in front of the stove. Immediately I couldn't help wondering if she had come prepared. I was the one who was unprepared. What was I getting myself into?

"You make everything in this place look cheap by comparison," I said.

Surprised, Caitrin whirled and the thin dress hesitated before doing the same. I managed to get a good look at a pair of long, tanned legs before the filmy skirt settled back to block the view.

"I hope that's a compliment. If it isn't, I can still skin you alive." She picked up the k-bar, still in its sheath.

"That won't be necessary until after I've eaten the breakfast you're making. I know when to hide my true intentions."

Caitrin put her hands on her hips and glared. "Sit down, shut up, and eat before I change my mind."

Humbled, I did as I was told. No doubt Caitrin could cook. The bacon was just the way I liked it, crisp, but not too. Even the fake eggs tasted almost as good as real. I had to ask. "What did you do to the eggs?"

She made a show of picking up her k-bar and brandishing it in my direction. "Is that a prelude to a complaint?"

"Only if you want it to be. What did you put in the fake eggs?"

"Nothing I'm going to be telling you about. My secret ingredients cannot be revealed. I checked the fridge. You're out of real eggs. Where did you come up with them the other day?"

I couldn't remember the last time a woman sat across the breakfast table. Especially one that hadn't spent the night in my bed. I wouldn't be telling her that, though. "I can't reveal all of my secrets or you'll leave me in the dust. Do you have any plans for the rest of the day?"

One thing I wouldn't be doing was showing her where my chickens laid their eggs.

"Besides getting home before it gets dark? Not especially. Why?"

"I want to do some scouting. If you want, you could help me. If you have the time, that is."

"Will I have to change?" she asked.

"Only if you want to be able to wear that dress for me again." This was moving far too fast for my liking.

Caitrin got up, grabbed her bag, and walked to my room at the end of the hall. Was it on purpose, or was it was just another room to her?

While I waited, I stretched out on the sofa. My eyes closed for what I thought was only a minute. I woke to Caitrin standing over me. The shotgun's barrel poked and jabbed. Startled, I jumped up and almost knocked her over.

She beat a retreat and sat down in front of the fireplace. At least she hadn't pulled the trigger in fear and panic.

Caitrin was dressed for the hunt. The k-bar was back in place on her belt. The double-barreled shotgun lay across her front, breach open. The strap crossed between her breasts, emphasizing them. I tried not to stare too long. I tried not to wonder if it was on purpose. "You're ready. Give me a couple and I will be, too."

"You were having a nightmare."

She must have heard me tossing and turning. I couldn't deny it. I was still sweaty and slightly uncomfortable. "I was. Yesterday was quite a shock to my system. You showed yourself and it wasn't to eat breakfast in my cul-de-sac. Our government visitor at the end of the street didn't help matters. Today will be a better day."

"I hope so. What's the plan?"

"We're going hunting," I admitted.

She looked surprised. "Really? For what?"

I explained the collapsible dipstick, the paint can and the markings to be left on each vehicle we'd be checking. With two of us to do the work, I could cover a lot more ground than if by myself.

The extra weight of a passenger, even one as light as Caitrin, slowed the pace of the electric bicycle, but not by much. At the first car, I showed her how to break open the cover and slide the measuring stick into the gas tank. She marked the fuel door to show how much remained, and then we would move on to the next.

Once she had the hang of it, we split up and covered twice the territory. We'd meet back at the intersection where we started, and I would mark the map with the separate routes we took and the quantities of fuel left behind.

Before long, I was riding ahead to open a line of tanks for her. She'd walk the line, measure and cap and then mark the results. We did about a hundred cars and trucks and discovered more fuel than I had storage for.

Our shadows were getting longer beneath the sun. "It's getting late in the day. I think it's time to get you home."

"I'm ready. I'm exhausted from getting on and off the bike," she said.

"You helped me a lot, Caitrin. It's no wonder. Do you trust me enough to take you, or do you want to find your way from here?"

"I've already made my decision about that. You're going to take me home."

"Mine?" My huge grin only encouraged Caitrin to roll her eyes. "All right then. Climb on for the last time."

Caitrin was all smiles when she threw a leg over for her ride. Even the shotgun digging uncomfortably into my back couldn't take away from the day's accomplishments. "I really enjoyed having you along. Maybe we can do it again soon." I could only hope.

"It's nice having someone else to talk to after all these months," she said.

Someone else. There it was. I let the slip pass unnoticed. She was getting comfortable in my presence. "If you want, I can pick you up and we can roam around looking for whatever it is you need to make your place more livable."

"That would be good. There's lots I need for the winter coming up.

I suspected she wouldn't let me take her all the way home, and I was right. She asked me to pull over and started to explain. I held up my hand. "It's not necessary. I understand. If it was the other way around, I'd do the same."

"Thank you, Russell." She kissed me on the cheek. "I had a great day."

"We both did, I'd say."

Caitrin blushed. She turned and fast-trotted toward an alley. She turned and waved. I pointed the bike toward my own home.

The day left me with plenty to think about. It had been a huge shock to come upon Caitrin waiting patiently at my door. When the truck arrived and she disappeared, I thought she left for good. That she took her chances and ran indoors to avoid detection shocked me.

It pleased me she trusted me enough to spend the night. I still had no idea if we would make a team. For now, I would run with it and see what might develop.

Once home, I unlocked the door and went around the interior, checking the curtains were closed before firing up the generator. The doors to the closet in my bedroom were open. Caitrin's bright cheery dress hung on a hanger.

I couldn't stop smiling as I washed off the day's accumulated grime. I put a potato in the microwave and threw some spices into a batch of chicken before putting it on the hotplate to simmer. Just for fun, I checked my watch and set the time on the microwave before stretching out on the sofa.

The explosions in my dream turned into pounding. Something was pounding on the roof. Wait. No. Not the roof. Confused, I rolled over and fell off the sofa. It woke me enough to recognize the sound.

In the dark, late at night, I refused to turn on the lights. Instead, I stumbled to the door. Without thinking, I opened it wide. I didn't even have a baseball bat within easy reach.

Caitrin must have heard me turn the lock. In her haste, she burst through the door and almost knocked me down. Reacting to her panic, I slammed the door shut behind her and locked it. "You scared the hell out of me.

What's going on?"

She couldn't talk. She couldn't catch her breath. Huffing and puffing, she must have run all the way from her place. I left her to calm down and regain a semblance of sanity while I went to check on dinner. She followed and watched carefully while I set another place at the table.

Not a word came out of her.

"It looks and sounds like you need a dose of reality. Sit down and take your time. While I wait, perhaps you can fill your stomach and figure out what you want me to know."

I ignored the fresh cuts and bruises on her face as I had ignored them the day before.

11

Russell and Caitrin

Caitrin paced back and forth between the kitchen and the hallway.

I let her go on until she slowed and caught her breath. The look of panic slowly began morphing into one of relief. I convinced her to sit in front of my plate while I pretended to ignore her by putting another potato in the microwave.

She devoured everything in front of her and pushed back from the table. The only thing she didn't do was ask for more. "Remind me never to get in the way when you're really hungry."

She worked the bandolier over her head in silence. She slid the plate out of the way and replaced it with her shotgun. The breach was closed.

I didn't ask if it was loaded. I figured, given the circumstances, that a measure of trust might be in order.

"Go wash up. You'll feel better, I promise. I'll stand guard." Over what, against what, I didn't know.

She wasn't forthcoming. She didn't move. She

continued to sit and stare. I wanted her in control.

"I'll still be here when you get back. Caitrin. Go."

Moving like an automaton, she disappeared down the hall. She left, or perhaps forgot, her shotgun on the table. Maybe after our day together, she had developed a measure of trust.

Water splashed in the bathroom.

She returned looking refreshed. Her hand covered the handle of the knife on her belt.

"It's your shotgun. I have no use for it."

Something had definitely spooked her. She was out after dark. That wasn't good.

"I'm sorry. I need to explain. After you dropped me off, I made my way home. I didn't take a direct route. I never do. After unlocking my door, I got quite a shock."

"Try to relax. Take your time. We have lots of it."

I sat across from her, and it looked like she was going to follow my lead.

She took two bites of dessert and then hesitated over the third. The fork clattered onto the plate. Her words tumbled out in a mad rush.

I listened, mouth agape, and put down my own fork.

She approached her place as she always did. Cautious. On the lookout for anything and everything. All of her watch-out signs and warnings were in place. None had been disturbed. No one had violated her privacy.

No one, that is, until she unlocked her door and walked into the mess that up to then had been her fortress. Disarray greeted her.

Contents of cupboards lay scattered on the floor.

Her furniture was cut open and searched.

Carpet was pulled up.

The bedroom was destroyed.

She knew, because exposed two-by-fours stared back from walls stripped of drywall.

Whoever tossed the place had done a job.

She didn't take the time to grab anything. Instead, she backed out without taking even one more step inside. She locked the door behind her and hot-footed it. She zigged and zagged, careful to check if anyone followed.

She stopped, waited, listened, peered around corners, backtracked and carried on, never moving in a straight line. Always she watched her back. Always she expected to be surprised at any moment.

It took hours to get anywhere close to my neighborhood.

Nothing and no one appeared to be following. As she got closer, she began to relax just a bit. When it came time to pound on my door in the dark, she went on heightened alert. Caitrin knew I'd be on alert, too.

When I opened the door without so much as a word, it shocked her into a panic attack.

She knew she'd be safe inside. She had an inkling in the back of her mind that she was taking a chance.

Would I even go to the door without knowing who was there? It was night, after all. She said her goodbye hours ago, in daylight.

Her story came out in a mad rush of words, hurried, as if she stopped to take a breath, she would forget what came next.

I offered up a solution, of sorts. It was a bottle of brandy.

I poured a shot. Caitrin gulped it down and asked for another.

I obliged, and she downed it just as fast.

"That's enough," I told her. "Go over to the sofa and

try to relax. I'm going to clean up."

I stuck my head around the corner to check on her. Eventually, the heat from the fireplace did its job. Her feet rested on the coffee table. I covered her with a blanket and sat beside her. She eased over. Her head ended up resting on my shoulder.

I arranged the blanket to cover both of us. I fell asleep waiting for the fire to die.

Water running in the bathroom roused me from a sound sleep. I wasn't accustomed to waking up so late in the day. I also wasn't accustomed to having company two days in a row.

Caitrin must have fired up the generator on her own. The only sounds I had grown accustomed to were my own. They didn't include a hairdryer doing its job on Caitrin's long, dark hair.

For some reason, that simple act on her part, that starting up the generator, pleased me. I began to think there might be some hope for us to work together more often.

She must have rummaged around in my room, because she came out wearing an old t-shirt. A pair of tanned, long legs hung out from the bottom of the thigh-length shirt.

She caught me looking for longer than I probably should have. She pulled the shirt even lower over her thighs and I blushed.

"Don't you be getting any ideas," she told me. "It's been too long since I last relaxed in safety. That's what I want to do today."

It pleased me to know we'd be spending more time

together. "That's all right. Whatever look you're going for, you've captured it. I've missed that, too. I'll tell you what. I'll change the sheets for you, and tonight you can crash in my bed."

She raised an eyebrow. "Will I be alone in there?"

"That's up to you."

"Then there's no sense in changing those sheets just yet," she replied.

I would have grinned like someone who just won the lottery, but for the fact there was no place to spend the money. Instead, I grinned like a fool. I didn't even try to hide it.

"And stop grinning."

I couldn't. Instead, I turned away and put on the coffee.

In the back of a closet, I rummaged through a pile of board games the previous occupants had for their kids. For the rest of the night and well into the next, we competed for the best properties and tried to stay out of jail.

She helped in the kitchen by brushing against me from time to time.

I didn't move away and neither did she when I did the same.

We flirted constantly.

Strip poker was out of the question. Whether on purpose or not, Caitrin made it quite evident that she had absolutely nothing on under the shirt.

When we tired of the board games, we talked. We talked long into the night and well into the early morning. We realized there would be no going back to the world we knew before the purges. We knew too there was bound to be more people just like us, whether single or living in groups.

There had to be, otherwise Caitrin's place would have remained untouched.

We also knew they might not be law-abiding. Knew they might not be friendly. That they might not be so willing to help others in the same situation. That they might want to loot and steal everything we had collected up to now and take it for their own.

It took until just before sunup to talk it out and come up with a partial solution. We were just about dead in our tracks from fatigue and nervous exhaustion.

Neither of us slept on the sofa.

I adjusted a corner of my bedroom blind to allow daylight into the room. I don't think either of us was disappointed by what we saw.

Hands and fingers and mouths and lips wandered feverishly.

We slept and woke up and started all over again.

The bed didn't get changed for a couple of days.

In between waking up multiple times next to a warm body firm in all the right places, Caitrin and I agreed to work together.

First on the list was expanding the number of safe houses and goods over the next months.

We thought we would need an additional three or four places in different neighborhoods. They had to be far apart from each other. We'd outfit them just like mine. At a moment's notice, we would be able to go on the run.

You could call them safe houses, I guessed.

By the time we finished developing a basic plan, we

knew it would take months to get everything set up. And that was if we could find the right locations equipped with fresh water reserves. If we didn't locate those places right off, it would take us even longer.

It didn't take much convincing to agree on the need for two trucks.

We'd need radios to stay in contact.

Maybe even a dog with a good nose to sniff out danger. At least we were thinking of danger, even if we weren't prepared for it beyond a couple of shotguns and a knife.

By late afternoon, we managed to drag ourselves out of bed and head for the shower. Our excuse, such as it was, was that we were saving water.

We joyfully wasted more than we saved.

Caitrin climbed on the bike behind me and we took off. We began slowly working our way to her place. To throw anyone off who might be watching, we worked the streets off the main drags and zig-zagged as though we were scouting gasoline reserves.

We arrived in the early afternoon to a wide-open front door.

"This isn't right. I locked it before I left. I'm sure of it," she said

I sensed panic in her voice. My own alarm bells started to ring. I suspected there were things Caitrin hadn't been forthcoming about, and probably even more she didn't want me to know. I thought I knew why. I pushed it into the background and concentrated on right now.

I went around the back of the house. Someone made

sure to fill the pool with all manner of things. Food. Canned goods. Chairs. Tables. They'd tossed it all in. It seemed like a jealous boyfriend had wanted to send a message.

"If there's anything you need in there, you better collect it. I won't be bringing you back here. You'd be wise to keep away."

She started to close the door. Not a good idea, considering how she'd found it.

"If you do that, whoever it was will know you returned."

"You're right. Let's just go."

She climbed on and we backtracked on our route. At a safe distance from her house, I stopped at a small, tree-covered park. "We need to talk."

Caitrin fished through her backpack and pulled out sandwiches. "I'm not completely useless."

"I never thought you would be."

Maybe not, but she was trying too hard. I took my time pouring coffee from the thermos. It was the last thing I could do to delay the inevitable. "Who was staying with you, Caitrin?"

She hesitated. Her eyes moved in every direction but mine.

I had all the time in the world.

She did too, until she didn't.

"My boyfriend."

Finally. Her admission wasn't a complete surprise. I wanted to know if he was an actual boyfriend, or someone she only hooked up with for convenience—hers, not his. "For how long?"

"Since before the purges," she replied.

So he was her boyfriend. That was good to know,

even at this late date.

"He's been getting weirder and weirder in the last months. I think he might have found a cache of drugs. He wanted to move us back into the center of the city. Why, I don't know. He wouldn't tell me."

It seemed to me like the two of them had a knock-down, drag-out fight, judging by what had been deposited into the pool. One, or both, had stomped off when they didn't get their way. And there were those bruises. I'd noticed them on her body. I didn't say anything, but she knew. How could she not?

"So you two had a fight and you took off back to my place?" I asked.

"No. Not at all. When I left, the place was just as neat and tidy as it always was. I was alone there for a couple of days. And yes, we had a fight, but that was a week ago. Konnor took off and I thought I wouldn't see him again. In fact, I was certain of it."

She wasn't so certain now. For all I knew, the poor chump could have eyes on us and neither of us would be the wiser.

"Well, we're into it now. What do you want to do, Caitrin?"

If she was smart, she'd recognize there was safety in numbers. And if she was real smart, she'd know I was definitely hooked on her. Hell, even I knew that, and I was one of the dumbest guys on the face of the earth when it came to women. Perhaps by now, I was the last one.

"Will you take me back to your place? I feel safe there."

There it was. Who was I to question it?

"Then let's get going."

Caitrin helped push the bike into the garage, and then I began the speech I rehearsed on the ride to my house. To our house, now.

I rehashed last night's conversation. I reminded her about what we decided. I explained that from now on, we would need to be more careful about our safety if we were going to be a team. We needed radios to stay in touch. We needed vests, and unfortunately, more guns.

We would have to increase the number of safe houses we could relocate to if need be. They wouldn't have to be anything fancy. They'd be temporary, only used if we had to hide out. We could shift from one to the other at random to stay in hiding.

We would begin it all by searching for the ideal trucks.

I led her to the map pinned on the wall in one of the spare rooms. It covered a radius of forty or fifty miles. It had roads, rivers, railways, power lines, waterways and lakes, everything we needed to know, plainly marked. I pointed out where we could move to if we had to.

She didn't think it wise until we did a recon of each of the areas.

She was right, and so I agreed.

And that's what we did over the next ten days. We located two half-tons with good rubber and loaded them to the tailgates.

We kept in touch with two-way radios.

We did our recons.

We locked suitable locations into the GPS and marked them on our paper maps.

Through it all, we got to know each other better.

It surprised both of us how easily we got along. At the end of the day, if we weren't too exhausted, we'd pick a movie from a cache of old black and white DVDs about the end of the world.

Sometimes, we would fall asleep on the sofa. One or the other would wake and we'd stumble off to bed to make frenzied love, or, more often, fall into exhausted sleep.

After suffering through months of loneliness, it was a good feeling to finally have a sense of routine with someone other than myself. Waking up in a nice warm bed didn't hurt, either. Caitrin turned out to be a willing lover, eager to please.

Perhaps it was all too easy, but even if it was, I welcomed it. I enjoyed it, even.

I wasn't so sure about Caitrin. I was beginning to sense she was becoming distant. I didn't say anything through her long periods of silence. When I had a question, it seemed like it took her forever to come up with a response. "Is there something I need to know? What's going on?"

"I want to go back to the house."

"Your old place?" I asked.

"That's the one."

"We'll saddle up first thing in the morning." I had in mind a quick trip there and back for her.

"No, I'm going alone," she insisted. "There's something I have to do."

I wanted to know why. I wanted to know what was left for her there. I wanted to know why I couldn't take her. I didn't ask those or the dozen other questions I had.

"I won't be long. I'll leave first thing in the morning. I'll make sure to be back before dark," she promised.

While Caitrin geared up, I tried one last time to convince her to let me take her on the bicycle. She insisted on going alone, and she insisted on walking.

In the end, I wasn't surprised at her stubbornness. I knew her too well by now.

"I'll see you tonight," she said.

She allowed me to check her gear.

When I was satisfied, I pulled the hoodie over her head and smacked her rear, hard.

She turned back at the door and grinned. She rubbed at her rear in the tight jeans.

"I'll get you for that."

"Only if you go back to those ratty old overalls."

I closed the door behind her, locked it, and went to the window. I pulled up the curtain. She disappeared around a corner without looking back, just as she did all those weeks before we met.

I let the curtain drop and wondered what I could do to take my mind off of my concerns. I had become quite attached to the woman in the short time we'd been together. She was reluctant to tell me much about her life before we hooked up. I didn't have a problem with that. I only wondered how long we'd last.

Even though we were alone, I knew she had the ability to take care of herself, even if she wouldn't admit it.

I went to the garage and readied the trailer with an empty drum and the pump. There was still plenty of gas to collect, and empty 55-gallon drums to fill. I checked the curtains and the doors and headed out to a new area I hadn't yet mapped.

There weren't a lot of vehicles, but most had plenty of fuel. I had the drum filled by noon, and made for home. Just as I rolled into the garage, the battery died. I fired up the generator and used the forced break to make lunch.

I didn't stop worrying.

12

A team of two

Waiting, alone and in the dark, had me nearly at wit's end. There was only so much I could do to keep busy. I did learn one thing while I waited, though.

I missed Caitrin at every moment.

The key scraped in the lock.

I jumped up from the sofa and bounded to the door like a puppy happy to see anyone.

Caitrin hurried through the door and I locked and barred it behind her.

She motioned for me to follow her into the kitchen. Without saying so much as a word, she attacked the Velcro on her vest with a vengeance. Fingers slipped and grabbed as she wrenched it back, making its customary zipping sound.

"Help me," she commanded.

Had she been attacked and beaten by her boyfriend again?

Knifed?

Shot?

I made a grab for the vest. It almost slipped out of my hands. I tightened my grip and heaved it onto the table. The vest landed with a heavy thud.

Caitrin ripped open a pocket. "Take a look."

Gold. The pocket was filled with shiny gold bars. Judging by the weight, the vest had to be filled with gold.

"Where did you find it?"

I opened the pockets, one at a time. Bars in a variety of sizes and weights slipped out and clattered onto the table.

"I've had the gold almost since the beginning. I stumbled on it months ago in a basement of one of the houses I raided."

"You know what this means, right?"

The magnitude of the discovery wasn't lost on either of us. "With all that gold we'll be able to buy our way out of just about anything."

Caitrin was right. And showing up with her gold meant she had both of our interests at heart. She'd committed, finally. We could begin our final preparations to leave the city behind.

I took her hand and led her down the hall to the bedroom. I flipped on a battery light.

"What's that on your shirt?"

She pulled it out and looked down before starting to unbutton it

"I must have spilled something."

She opened her shirt, exposing bare breasts. She pulled my face between them. Her scent was strong.

I thought I detected a hint of something else.

"I need a shower, she said. "Are you coming?"

We drove the trucks north toward the mountains, still in exploration mode. Still looking for places to use as safe houses or to settle into. At the half-way point on the side of a hill, I halted and waited for Caitrin to catch up. I took out a map and unfolded it on the hood.

"Why are we stopping?" she asked.

"Check our ground. We've been here before. Something is telling me to avoid where we've been. In any case, this is still pretty close to the city."

"Do you think there could be others around?" she asked.

"Yes. The question is, do we want to cross paths with any of them? I think it's still too early in the game for that. What do you think?"

She took her time answering. She walked to the edge of the road and looked down at what we were in such a hurry to leave behind. She was proving hesitant to move out of her comfort zone.

Hell, I was too. "We've been lucky so far, Caitrin. We've scouted around quite a bit. We haven't crossed paths with anyone. If anything, that would have put us in the cross-hairs of anyone looking for trouble."

"That's all true." Caitrin considered her reply. "We would have looked pretty organized to anyone who had a yen to take it all."

"I have to admit, we're pretty comfortable down there. We both contributed a lot of work these past weeks. We'll be able to go back to our stockpiles any time we want." I hoped that would make it easier, knowing we could always return. Our labors wouldn't end up being abandoned.

"You're right. It will be a fresh start. Another one."

I agreed, but I was starting to wonder. "I don't think

it's going to be the last."

I covered Caitrin's hand with my own and tried to reassure her. It would be difficult for both of us to start from scratch yet again. At the same time, I knew it was best to get out of the city.

I opened her door and waited. For a split second, I thought she might turn back.

"I'm with you, partner," she said.

With the sun low over the horizon, we crested a hill overlooking a valley. It was populated everywhere with tents. In all colors. Every outdoor store in the city must have been raided and this was where they ended up. It looked like a Rainbow City. It stuck in my mind, and that's what I called it.

I had to slow for a sharp bend in the highway. It was that, or dump the truck in the ditch along with the trailer when I went off-road. Several hundred yards beyond, I was forced to a complete stop by a series of cement barricades that had been placed across the roadway. Anyone wanting to get past would have to zig-zag their way through.

I halted short of entering and waited for Caitrin. The sight of so many tents meant lots of people to go along with them. Too many people. We looked at each other, growing more uncomfortable by the minute.

We'd been alone and on our own for a long time. Our discomfort at the thought of having to interact with such a large community forced us to hesitate.

"What do you think?"

Caitrin didn't stop and think. Her response was immediate. "I think we should backtrack out of here. The sooner, the better."

Decision made, the concrete barricade presenting itself in front of us turned out to be the least of our worries. Heavy trucks jockeyed into position behind us to block any chance we might have to back up and turn around. We could neither advance nor retreat on the narrow highway.

If I was worried before, now I was terrified about an ambush. I didn't see the armed men walking out from cover on the side of the road.

Caitrin did.

"We have company."

She moved closer and closed her shotgun. The weapons the men carried were slung by their sides. It was somewhat of a relief, but I was certain it was only temporary.

"We're into it now. This is going to take some talking," I said.

They appeared friendly enough. They weren't threatening. Their weapons never pointed in our direction. They tried very hard to convince us to go in and look at the encampment.

"We need to talk about it in private," I told the men.

Caitrin and I pretended to discuss the pros and cons of a visit to the encampment. Following what we thought was a reasonable amount of time, I approached the spokesman to advise him we had to decline their invitation. It was the only decision we could make for our own safety and security.

I thanked him, and we ended up talking for a bit. I learned that at least another half-dozen communities had sprung up in the hills in the wake of the purges. The residents remained camped out, waiting until they felt the time was right to take over the abandoned small towns scattered in the hills. With winter coming, they would have to act soon.

The men pointed out a series of what I called Rainbow Cities on our map. Through casual conversation we learned there were many other places even farther north. It made sense. The isolation was perfect for the growing numbers of preppers who never thought about acquiring property to practice what they preached.

Finally, our talk ended. At a signal from a sentry, the trucks blocking our retreat moved off. We were allowed to turn around.

We didn't waste time getting away.

We high-tailed it back into the city in the dark of night as fast as we could. Headlights blazed our trail. When we finally stopped, we were back at the home and the double garage we were so familiar and comfortable in. Even Caitrin didn't balk at spending one more night so close to her former boyfriend.

Our trip into the hills had us even more concerned for our well-being than before we left. Nervous and exhausted, we climbed into the bed we shared and slept like the dead.

Or the purged.

Never once did we talk about traveling all that way in the dark with our headlights on.

13

Still a team

The gunshot thundered through the night and echoed off the houses in the cul-de-sac. I tore out of bed and ran to the living room. I flipped open a corner of the curtain to be confronted by the night's own dark curtain. There was nothing to see. I rushed to check the locks on the front and back doors before collecting our firearms.

I returned to the bedroom to find Caitrin only partially dressed. "What's going on? What's happening?"

"I couldn't see anything. I'm not venturing outside in the dark to find out. Neither are you. We'll wait for daylight," I said.

We had a morning routine following breakfast. We dressed together, each checking the other's equipment. We had to be sure we had everything we would need if we crossed paths with anyone.

Shotgun at the ready, I exited the house first. After a quick check, I gave Caitrin our all-clear signal and she followed.

It took a couple of minutes before we recognized what must have happened. At the exit to the cul-de-sac, a body lay on the ground next to a shotgun. Caitrin gasped and collapsed against me. I wasn't quick enough, and she went to her knees.

"Is that Konnor?"

"Yes."

I pulled her up and pushed and pulled and almost had to drag her back to the house. "We're leaving here as soon as we can get our gear together."

"I should bury him," she said.

The man shouldn't be here, but that was old news now. He found out where Caitrin was living and made sure to punish her for her transgressions against him, real or imagined. She'd been right. He was sick after all.

"I'll do the burying while you do the preparations," I told her.

"If it wasn't for him, I don't think I would have survived."

"In that case, you have something good to remember about him, wouldn't you say?" I asked.

Caitrin didn't respond.

Grave-digging was a new one on me.

I laid out a plastic sheet and rolled the body on top of it.

I dragged her former boyfriend's body into a back yard and went in search of a shovel. There was no way I'd be using one of ours.

By the time I finished, I had quite a sweat going on.

The best I could hope for was I'd never end up a cemetery grave-digger. Who would I be burying, besides the one I just did?

There was no one left.

Following our encounter with the tent towns on our exploratory excursion into the northern hills, we were happy to be back home and on familiar ground. Unfortunately, thanks to Caitrin's former boyfriend's suicide, any chance we had of remaining here was stolen from us by the crazy man.

There was no question we were most familiar with the city. Caitrin was even a city girl, having grown up in it. I was the newcomer, but by now, even I had gotten to know a lot of the nooks and crannies that allowed me to survive on my own.

As a team, Caitrin and I were definitely becoming more secure. Why chance breaking it up by moving to somewhere unfamiliar? That would mean new challenges, many that wouldn't be recognized right away. Back in those hills, with winter coming on, it would soon be snowing. Where would people find the food they needed if they became snowed in?

I didn't want to contemplate it. I definitely didn't want to be a part of it.

We had a narrow escape in the hills. We were lucky the group we encountered was friendly. It could have worked out much worse. Back where we started, we had nothing but time to make good with what we already had in place.

Until Konnor, in his madness, screwed everything up.

Caitrin had everything stowed away by the time I patted down the dirt with the back of the shovel and returned.

"Is it finished?" she asked.

"Yes." I didn't have any more words.

Breakfast was on the table. I wasn't exactly in the mood for food. I needed to prepare for the long day ahead. Exhausted from my efforts at digging the hole in the hard, dry ground, I ate fast.

"Good. You're eating, too. You need to know I can't stay here now," she confessed.

"I know you can't. I'm not unsympathetic, you know. We'll leave as soon as we can."

The map case was sitting on the table, and Caitrin had taken out one of the border with Mexico.

"What's with the maps? What are you thinking?"

She pointed to the Mexican border. Her finger stopped on Tecate.

I gave her a puzzled look. "And?"

"What if all that's been going on is only happening in this country?"

I had to admit I never thought to turn on a radio the whole time I'd been living in the house. It never occurred to me. Even in the truck I streamed recorded music.

"We're going to spend one last night here, I said. "We can talk about it this afternoon."

I lit a fire. Its heat, together with our own fevered lovemaking, caused us to forget all about the events of the day. Caitrin's warm body felt good against mine. By firelight, it looked pretty good, too.

Our troubles disappeared, even if only temporarily.

I left Caitrin sleeping while I tip-toed out of the bedroom to search for an old analog radio stashed somewhere in the garage. It was a fact that none of our own digital radio or television stations were transmitting. Mexico was not that far away. Perhaps their antiquated radio stations might still be broadcasting on the AM or FM bands.

The batteries checked out and I set the receiver on

scan. Caitrin was right. Music. And voices. And plenty of chatter in Spanish.

I couldn't contain myself. I ran into the bedroom and yanked the covers off the bed. I hesitated, letting my eyes roam over the tanned, naked woman sprawled on her back in my bed. I contemplated climbing in beside her where I knew she'd welcome me with enthusiasm.

Instead, I sat on the edge of the bed. There was no time for us to waste. I placed the radio on the night table, turned up the volume, and waited for Caitrin to wake up.

We were going to be heading south, down Mexico way. I just knew it. Already I could picture us together on a beach on the Baja peninsula. My only question was, would it be the east side, or the west?

"What happened to my sheet?" she mumbled.

Caitrin stretched luxuriously on her back. Her eyes opened wide as she caught me out observing her naked body with a hungry look. Her eyes turned to sultry slits. She reached for me. Her legs parted and her feet slipped up on the bed. It was a sight I had never been able to say no to.

"Come down here. We don't have to leave right this instant, do we?"

Of course not.

14

New Challenges

Caitrin and I agreed we had to head south. What we didn't understand was how long it would take to come up with a plan. Once that was solved and we actually had a plan, we had to agree on it.

We had no idea the amount of stress that would cause.

We fought and argued and disagreed over just about everything, no matter how big or small.

The magnitude of the operation slowly began to dawn on us. It may even have caused the beginnings of a permanent rift, but we were too involved to recognize the possibility, concentrated as we were on making good our escape from the city.

An entire day and a night were dedicated to discussing our options for the trek south. It would be a giant undertaking, and not without risks.

We made lists.

Consulted our growing collection of maps.

Asked ourselves question after question.

We fought and argued and eventually ate if nerves

allowed for it. Then we went at it all over again.

Sleep wasn't an option for either of us. We needed to settle it, and we needed to settle it as soon as we could. Complete agreement wasn't necessary, but some form had to prevail.

Should we go direct, as fast as we could? Or should we use back roads and two-lane highways to avoid major metropolitan areas where there might still be patrols? And what about patrols? While neither of us had seen any recently, that didn't mean they weren't out there.

Our biggest obstacle to settling everything once and for all turned out to be routing. We argued about that long into the early morning. We got louder and louder in our insistence that it had to be one way, or the other.

It turned into, What's the point of either one of us being here if you're not going to listen?

It went on and on from there back to the beginning.

I was of a mind to make a run for it down a direct freeway route. It should be full speed ahead and damn the consequences. Caitrin was only pretending to listen. More surprising, she agreed to consider it.

Then, after several hours of back and forth on so many other things, she brought up her case yet again. She insisted we needed a more indirect approach for what was to be our run to the Mexican border.

The points she made were well-reasoned and sensible. And it did make sense, once I stopped to consider her proposal. There was a downside, though, and a pretty serious one. An indirect route at night would take a lot longer. We'd be driving two trucks, with no lights front or rear, on dark, isolated and unfamiliar roads while dragging trailers behind us.

How long it would take us was anyone's guess.

How could I not consider it? Caitrin turned out to be a valuable asset. Were it not for her, I'd still be wandering around the city in search of resources for the coming winter.

As it stood now, for weeks, all of our efforts were directed toward packing up and leaving the security of a familiar area. That was our safe house idea. We'd be surrendering plenty of resources to feed, clothe, heat and cool us into eternity.

Perhaps it sounded too good to be true, but it was the truth. And the truth had become plainly obvious to both of us. Notwithstanding the discovery of the settlements in the northern hills, we were pretty much alone in the city.

We could only hope we would be alone on our trek, as well.

Getting out of the city would eat up the first night. Perhaps even the better part of two nights while we familiarized ourselves with driving at night. That was another thing. We wouldn't be able to use headlights. How would we navigate in complete darkness?

It would be a stretch to find a suitably isolated place to stop before day broke. We needed somewhere to park two loaded half-ton trucks out of sight of any military traffic or anything else that might still be on the roads.

As far as aerial night patrols, we'd have to take our chances. Infra-red cameras would have us standing out like beacons in the dark. We didn't know if they were still launching them, or if, in fact, they ever had. Drone aircraft flew high and were mostly undetectable.

Our trucks would need to be covered with camouflage netting during the daylight hours. We would have to sleep then, too, in the heat. Food wouldn't be a problem. We'd pre-cook enough meals to get us to the border and use battery-operated coolers to keep it good.

Then we'd tear it all down, pack up, and proceed for another night until doing the same thing all over again. In the dark.

A week? Two? We didn't know. We did know that it wouldn't be full speed ahead by any measure.

Down dark roads.

Through mountain passes. With drop-offs.

Limited speed.

Chance encounters.

All while dragging trailers.

At night.

Would there be others with the same intent? We didn't know, but judging by what we witnessed day after day in the city, we doubted it. We would be alone.

After all our talk, all the arguing, all the fighting, I ended up agreeing with Caitrin. A night trip it would be. I think I knew that from the very beginning, but I couldn't admit it, especially to her.

I came away convinced she could stand up for herself. Our disagreements convinced me.

The makeup sex in front of the fireplace was amazing. She was insatiable. It was as though she received a birthday present she longed for, and others might be on the way.

We had a plan. We knew where we were going. We knew when. It gave us all the time in the world to get outfitted. We took our time locating vehicles. They needed to get top mileage and have load capacity.

The ability to tow a trailer was an absolute necessity. We didn't think four-by-fours would cut it. Gas mileage would be poor. We wouldn't be dealing with snow or desert crossings. More likely, we'd encounter washouts. With a bit of luck, we could avoid them, or take the long way around.

We would haul our own gasoline and oil. The trucks would be equipped with solar panels and inverters to keep everything charged: electronics, comm radios, laptops. We decided to keep a digital record of our trials and tribulations. We made sure we had spare parts with everything compatible in the event of breakdowns.

In a month, we thought we were ready. By then we had checked lists, made new ones, discarded items only to add them later. It seemed to me we spent more time arguing about inconsequential items to be brought along, until one explained to the other the need for it.

In the end, it all worked out. The makeup sex was still hot and sweaty.

We were prepared.

A certain reluctance to act set in.

Were we doing the right thing? Everything we had was here, in the city. Unlimited resources. Freedom to move about at will. Everything.

It took almost a week to convince ourselves that we really were ready. We had a run of well over two hundred miles to the border, at night, to prove ourselves wrong.

What had we missed? What could go wrong?

If we never left, we would never find out.

Departure-day arrived.

We would embark on our trip as soon as it got dark. Our grand plan was to sleep during our final day.

It didn't come to fruition. Instead, we went for a walk in the park, holding hands like the lovers we had become.

It was a perfect sunny and warm day, filled with blue sky and hope for our future and a little sadness, too. We tramped through the tall grass and wildflowers growing like weeds in their unkempt state.

We made our way back to the familiar cul-de-sac where we first met and spent so much time together. The blackout curtains remained in place. Candles provided the light over which we shared a romantic dinner. The fireplace did its final duty and burned itself out, just as we did in front of it.

We got away late, closer to midnight than our planned departure time of first dark. We blamed it on the two bottles of wine we shared, rather than admit we were depressed about leaving everything we knew behind.

In all likelihood, there would be no coming back.

Our choice of vehicles performed flawlessly.

The twelve small, low power red and green LEDs I installed front and rear on trucks and trailers worked remarkably well. Whoever brought up the rear knew where the truck in front was. Ditto for when the driver in the lead looked in a mirror and saw the dim red and green front markers of the vehicle behind.

They were position lights only. They couldn't be used for illumination. I hadn't designed them that way. They were too tiny. They were programmed to blink front and back when brakes were applied. There was one disadvantage. If the lead drove off the road, the vehicle behind would most likely end up following it.

Thankfully, the clouds stayed away. The marine layer refused to descend. The waxing moon provided just enough light, if we drove slowly, to take us to the correct roads. Even so, I took a wrong turn. By the time I realized what happened, we traveled a good distance out of the way. Uncertain and needing to get my bearings, I halted to consult our map.

Caitrin hopped out of her truck. Between sobs and crying, she spent a good five minutes berating me.

I pretty much ended up doing the same thing—the frustrated crying, that is, not the berating. We were nervous about the trek in its beginning stages. We were upset about leaving the so-familiar city behind.

I tried reassuring her. I held her in my arms. I explained how the pressure on both of us to perform flawlessly on this part of our journey was immense. It was stressful to look out over the hood and not be able to see anything in front for more than a few feet.

By the time I admitted I'd screwed up the routing, dawn was an hour away. We pulled over on the southern outskirts of the city. We hoped to find shade in a bushy, treed park to halt for the day beneath the trees.

We were upset. We were tired and exhausted. We hadn't made our planned objective for the first night. We didn't bother with the camo netting. We were too tired. We didn't even eat. We fell into a nervous sleep in the truck cabs where we parked.

I woke first and roused Caitrin. Sometime during the day, she must have changed into short shorts and a see-though shirt. It looked too good on her. Rivulets of perspirations trailed into the deep vee of her breasts.

I was entranced and she knew it.

It didn't take much for her to entice me once she stripped off her clothes and lay back on the thick carpet of grass. I collapsed beside her and we made love. I picked green grass out of her hair while she went through the coolers looking for a bottle of wine she stashed for just such an occasion.

She looked too good bent over the back seat. Long legs covered in perspiration and firm naked breasts were too much to ignore.

"You just had me."

Was she annoyed? I couldn't tell. "Yes. And I want you again."

"Very well. I'm here, and I'm available." She was no slouch in the wanting department, either. Her thighs began their desperate, familiar shaking and we finished with one another.

There was no mistaking the effect the woman had on me.

I held her closer than she wanted. There was an unspoken tension that developed between us. She stepped away, out of my arms, and began putting on her clothes.

"Daylight in the swamp, sunshine. What did you make us for breakfast?" I asked, trying for a smile from her.

"Don't you mean nighttime in the swamp?" she asked.

I reached into a door pocket and offered up beef jerky. "I'm not sure of the best before date, but would you like some orange juice to wash it down, miss?"

"Two over, bacon crisp, and a steaming cup of coffee, por favor, would do nicely," she said.

"So that's why you wanted the learning Spanish DVD. You've been cheating on me."

"Si, señor. Buenos días. Como estas?"

It seemed like we didn't have a care in the world. We stole time to make hurried, sweaty love yet again on the grass in broad daylight. There wasn't a single soul to bear witness. Perhaps that was why we were so exuberant.

The sun was just beginning to set.

It was eerily quiet. Not even birds chirped. The end of the day stayed warm. Caitrin pulled on her shorts and tucked in her shirt.

Something, a faint sound, caught my attention.

I whispered to her to get to the other side of the truck where she kept her shotgun. The breech snapped closed and two clicks told me she'd cocked both sawed-off hammers. If there was someone spying on us, they were going to be in trouble.

My own pump was just out of reach. I eased toward the door and pulled out a map to cover my other hand. I flicked it open slowly. The pump was laying across the driver's seat. I reached for it as a flash of light glanced off the side window. Someone was watching us. Had they seen us making love?

"Someone's here. Can you see anything?" I asked.

She shook her head and swiveled it slowly as she donned the bandolier.

Three men walked into sight from behind the small shack near where we parked. They were laughing. And they were armed. Bandana-covered faces and dark glasses stared at us from beneath black hoodies.

For some reason, the first thing that occurred to me was they must be hot in all those clothes. In another instant I reached for the shotgun.

Caitrin's sawed-off boomed twice in quick succession. She aimed wide. A spray of shot kicked up sand beside the threesome. There was no danger to any of them.

She broke the action and reloaded, cocked and ready. I used the opportunity to haul out my shotgun. I aimed it dead center of the three hoodlums. They hadn't been smart enough to separate.

If worse came to worse and we fired again, we'd make mincemeat out of them. Either that didn't occur to them, or they didn't care. Maybe they were on drugs.

"What do you want?" I asked.

They continued their advance. "We want your trucks."

"You should leave us and go find your own," I said.

"Yours look pretty good. We're going to take them."

That was all it took. "You can't have our trucks." I fired and racked and fired again. The sound echoed off the walls of the nearby buildings. Caitrin pulled the trigger on both barrels. Her shots went wide. The recoil forced her back two steps. For an instant I wondered if she'd ever practice-fired her shotgun.

There was no time for anything more. Hesitation meant the three hoodlums would be on us, and death or worse would be sure to follow. I couldn't take the chance they would leave us with anything. All of our plans would go up in smoke.

I fired three more times. Two collapsed and lay still. The third raised a hand and pointed at Caitrin. "She she's the one—"

Caitrin raised her shotgun and leaned in. A double-barreled blast sent the man to the ground. He died still trying to speak while pointing at Caitrin.

There was no sense checking for a pulse on any of them. There was nowhere to take them. No one to call. Our first aid supplies weren't capable of handling men on the way to being dead, if they weren't already.

Caitrin approached the bodies, shotgun at the ready. She only halted when she was overtop all three. "You can't have our trucks. We told you that. Why didn't you listen?"

It was too late. We'd done all the damage we could in the belief that if we didn't, strangers would do it to us.

"Let's get packed up, Caitrin. We need to get out of here as fast as we can."

The camo netting we ended up finally stringing wasn't built for a quick getaway. It took too much time to remove and stow. By then, motorcycles rumbled in the distance. We managed to get half the nets stowed. We left the remainder in a pile on the ground.

"It's time. We need to get out of here right now," I insisted.

I dragged the netting over the bodies.

An hour later in the night, we were back on our planned route and out of the suburbs.

We modified our stopping point based on the previous night's mileage. We became accustomed to our marker light system. We made good time. We planned on paved roads, and that's what we had. Mile after mile of gray, sun-bleached, two-lane asphalt made it easy to see by the light of the moon.

By the time daylight threatened to envelop us on our second night, we were ready. The previous night had been our test, in more ways than we wanted it to be. Piling up bodies wasn't in our plan. Our experience told us we were the only ones left. Now we knew we weren't and would have to keep a lookout.

The spare netting went up without a hitch. We ate sandwiches and salad from the coolers. A little wine washed it all down. We bedded out beneath the shade of the net and tried to forget about the day before.

If we were lucky, the next night would prove us right to have chosen a run to the border under cover of darkness.

We'd been smart to plan the drive over the hills in a waxing moon. Caitrin hadn't wanted to at first. She felt it would make us vulnerable if anyone was out and about in the dark. Once we got into the hills, she saw for herself that it was the right thing to do. In complete darkness, the driving would have been even more treacherous.

We slowed when tall trees blocked the moonlight. We rode the brakes on downhill runs, fearful one or the other vehicle would get away from us and run off the road in the too-invisible sharp curves and steep banks.

Occasionally we passed barriers that had been crashed through. Whether there were others that had chosen to do the moonlit midnight cruise ahead of us, we didn't know. We didn't care.

We were only glad to be on our own.

15

Crossing a line

On our second night, fatigued beyond belief, we halted early. Driving without lights on the mountain roads did us in. Still, we weren't that far off our schedule.

We camped in a small clearing we marked in advance on our maps. It turned out to be surrounded by an expanse of trees. That alone made it a perfect place to disappear once we drove the trucks as deep as we could into the woods.

A gentle wind rustled branches. Leaves whispered their response. The moon winked in and out between the swaying branches. The sound was hypnotic, almost resembling white noise, washing away memories of the fatal encounter on the edge of the city.

Our spirits were high, though. We ended up making good time, all things considered.

"We could stay here," Caitrin said.

"We could, yes. But we won't." How nice it would be if only.

"We don't know what's around the next bend," Caitrin said.

"No, we don't."

"There could be zombies," she said, and laughed nervously.

"There could. But we can handle them. We already took care of three."

Caitrin disappeared behind the truck. I caught sight of her, naked but for her boots. Her white body almost shone in the moonlight.

She laughed and rushed down a trail lined with trees and bushes. She yelled and disappeared. "Catch me if you can."

A loud splash followed. I hurried to undress and chase after her, a lot slower than I wanted. She really had disappeared. Splashing in the lake I didn't know existed gave her away. Caitrin huffed and puffed and rolled around in the small lake.

"How did you know this was here?" I asked.

"I heard the water lapping against the shore with the wind. Isn't it great?"

We splashed and swam and laughed, delighted for the change and a chance to get clean again.

"I missed our shower," she said.

"I thought so. I still remember the look on your face when I told you I had running water. After your shower, when you joined me in the kitchen, you looked amazing."

"I didn't look so amazing before the shower? So that's why you were staring at me." She smiled.

"Yeah. You clean up pretty good. And I was more worried that you'd claim squatter's rights and use your shotgun on me. Sometimes I still wonder what you saw in me."

"I wonder the same about you. Come on. Let's go back to camp. I'm getting cold," she said, shivering.

"I noticed."

Caitrin was too slippery to hang onto. Instead, we strolled hand in hand down the trail toward the trucks. I pinched her rear and she giggled.

"Wait. What was that? Did you hear it?" She stopped dead in her tracks and went down to a crouch.

I leaned in close. "Shh. Listen. Dammit we don't even have clothes."

We squatted behind a low bush on the edge of the clearing. Our trucks appeared undisturbed.

"Is there someone there? We should have taken a gun with us. We could lose it all," I said.

"The doors are still closed—wait, look. Over there." She pointed toward the highway we exited to get into the shelter of the small clearing. "It's a convoy."

Mostly half-tons and a single VW Beetle chugging along made up the bulk of the vehicles. The convoy went past the turnoff and didn't slow.

"The trucks look too small to be military. Do you think it could be people like us?" I asked.

We waited for them to disappear before walking the rest of the way to our campsite.

"We got lucky. They could have pulled in here, too. I wonder if they're only traveling at night like us?" I handed Caitrin her shotgun. I checked my own and donned the bandolier.

"We're getting careless after our success at getting out of the city alive with our trucks. We need to be more careful out here. By the look of it, there's a lot more people with the same idea."

"I agree. Now let's try to get some sleep. Tomorrow is probably going to be another scorcher," I said.

Sleep was fitful in the heat of the day. We woke to worry and make sweaty, rushed love and worry some more while washing up with a swim in the lake. By sunset, we were ready to get back on the road.

We took turns going back to the small lake to wash dishes and get ready for what we expected would be the final night of our trek.

It was a tossup who was more excited to have our destination so close.

We could almost taste victory, even though we weren't in competition with anyone but ourselves.

It was well past midnight. I pulled to the side of the road and halted. Caitrin stopped behind me. I waved and pointed. "Look. There it is."

Tecate was hard to miss. It presented a dull glow against the dark horizon. Much like the few Mexican towns I'd seen, at night they didn't compare to even a small American town of the same size for being lit up.

"We'll pull off the road if we can and wait until the sun comes up. If it looks good, we'll get a bit of shuteye, too. I don't think we should bunk out in the same cab. Just in case," I said.

"You're right. Now that we're almost there, I wouldn't want to lose half of our hard work to a thief," she replied.

We bedded down for the remainder of the night.

I arose refreshed and excited to have our destination so close.

Caitrin was stretched out in the cab of her truck, still sleeping, when I pulled out the binoculars for a better look at our future.

Tecate wasn't very big. I scanned the town, looking for the highway to the south. I took a look at the border crossing, then swept the binoculars east and west. A huge swath of ground was being worked with heavy equipment. Clouds of rising dust were swept away by the light wind. The ground was being stripped and leveled.

Both ends of the project, whatever it was, were being worked on at the same time. They looked to be working toward a common goal—the border crossing. I wondered if it was our new country preparing to close their borders to the gringo hordes descending upon it.

It occurred to me they were a bit late to the party. It must have been quite a while since there was anyone heading south any longer. Then I remembered the convoy. I put the glasses away and tapped on Caitrin's window.

"Rise and shine, cowgirl. It's time."

I pulled out a map and spread it on the hood while she rubbed the sleep out of her eyes.

She searched in the cooler and came up with a couple of bottled ice coffees. She popped the tops and handed one to me.

"We've come over two hundred miles. I can't believe it."

Caitrin set the drink on the hood and did a happy dance.

I joined her.

She twirled, exposing long, familiar legs beneath the filmy dress.

I didn't want the performance to end. Reluctantly, I

dragged her back to the map on the hood.

"We want Mexico 3 south. Once we enter, we'll head straight south, then jag to the left and do an immediate right. That should get us on 3. We need to fill up with gas, too."

"What will we use for money? Will they take our dollars, do you think?"

"We won't know until we try. I'd hate to have to use some of your gold. We'll eat it up pretty fast that way."

Would she even use it for the benefit of both of us? I wondered.

"We need to find a bank. Let's give that a try first," she said.

"Do you think? I'd bet that would set the wolves on us for sure."

"Maybe, but we can cruise all day and all night after we're across with full tanks. It shouldn't take us that long to get out of the way."

That was true. During all the night driving, it never occurred to me that once we crossed the border, we'd be able to drive all night with lights and all day, too.

"One more thing. The firearms. We're going to have to stash them. I'll do it before we cross."

We stretched out in the cabs. The windows were open against the heat. We'd been able to sleep through it until now.

Caitrin was first to wake up. She completely changed her look with another dress and shoes and only a bit of makeup. She wrapped a scarf around her neck and tucked it into her shirt, covering her naked breasts beneath.

"You look like a million dollars, girl," I told her. "I'm impressed."

"We're going to get checked out by the border guards.

I figure gringos like us need all the help we can get. I'll smile and show a little thigh if I have to. What do you think?"

"I'm in favor of whatever works. In the meantime, can I get a little of that thigh?" I joked.

"How about both of them?" She giggled and lifted the front of her dress. "How's that?"

"More than a little. I'll take it."

"All right then, pervie. Let's roll," she said.

There was one more thing. "Not yet. The weapons. Firearms and ammunition aren't allowed across the border."

"Should we stash them or ditch them?" she asked.

She had me with that. I didn't want to jeopardize our crossing, but if we were going to end up in a Mexican jail—

I never told her about the hiding places I installed on both trucks. "I have a plan. It includes me getting on my back and crawling beneath the trucks. Your job is to pass me the guns.

"While you're looking up my skirt." She laughed.

"Well, now that you mention it—"

I waited for Caitrin to make up her mind while I encouraged her by getting under a truck. As far as I was concerned, we were equals in this deal. If she said no—

"Let's go for it. What's the worst that can happen?" she asked.

"Bread and water for me. For you, not so much if you flash those thighs, girl."

"In that case, let's rock and roll, smuggler."

I was under too much pressure to even smile. "We're not smugglers. We're refugees. Remember to make that claim if you need to and we'll see how it goes. And you go first, smiley. Warm, tanned thighs and all."

Damn but she did look good.

16

La línea

With bravado gone and our next stop the border, Caitrin quickly turned into a nervous wreck at the prospect of crossing into Mexico and the unknown. Hell, we were both shaking, but it was more obvious with her. Her knees bounced. She cleared her throat and swallowed with a sound so dry I offered her my bottle of water.

We had one single thing to do. That was to get accepted into Mexico. When the border was behind us, we would be home free. From there, I was certain we'd find a tiny bit of sand on one coast or the other. It was all we would need to put down tent pegs until we got a more permanent palapa constructed.

We traversed two hundred and twenty miles of mountain road in the dark of night. Outside of the bandits we encountered on the edge of the city, and the scare from the convoy passing by our overnight campsite on the lake, we'd done it in good time.

So far, we hadn't driven off any cliffs.

My confidence in Caitrin had been well-placed. She

was capable and willing to try anything to get us to safety.

"Wait. There's something I need to tell you," I said.

"What now?" She sounded exasperated, impatient to get this over with as much as I was.

"You need to know I couldn't have done any of this without you."

Caitrin got out of the truck. She put her arms around me and we kissed. "I couldn't have done it without you, either. Now, can we get this circus on the road? I'm almost peeing my pants at the prospect of getting over the line before something bad happens."

"Don't feel all alone. I'm right there with you, minus the peeing in pants thing. Let's get going."

A VW Beetle pulled out of a turnout in front of us. We followed it to the crossing. I wondered if it was the same one that was part of the truck convoy that went past us in the night.

Caitrin rolled up to the border behind the couple in the rusted, beat-up Beetle.

The driver began a heated discussion with a border guard. As the conversation became more intense, the woman in the passenger seat tried to calm her partner. It wasn't working.

The woman sobbed hysterically. Her partner began swearing at the guards. Somehow, it didn't seem like the thing to do when you wanted to get into a foreign country.

In the small building, another guard said something into a portable radio. Seconds later, a military-green Humvee rolled up. Armed troops disembarked and the car was directed to a turnout. I prayed that the same thing wouldn't happen to us, even if I had no intentions to yell and scream at anyone.

I repeated my mantra for the day.

"Remember to smile, Caitrin. Remember to smile."

If talking out loud to myself would do any good, we'd be across in jig time.

Caitrin eased the truck and trailer up to the waiting guard. The blinking green light turned red. The guard waved to another inside the building. He brought out a permit of some sort and affixed it to Caitrin's windshield. He waved her through, and I sighed with relief.

She leaned out of the window and looked back at the car that had been pulled over in the turnout. The couple were still going at it.

Caitrin pointed across the street. I had no idea what she was pointing at.

The guard tapped on my hood and smiled.

It was my turn to go.

I kept my eyes on Caitrin's truck as I eased up to the building to wait for my permit.

A boom followed by a flash of orange and all manner of rubble descended on the street Caitrin had only just traversed. I lost sight of her truck in the smoke and dust floating across the street.

The guard began running in the direction of the rubble. His compadre in the office ran out to join him as they double-timed it toward the remains of a former building. Cement blocks and rubble blocked the street.

Through the yelling in a language I didn't understand, I heard the word banco repeated again and again. And then I saw the only thing left hanging on the front of the building. The sign said Casa de cambio.

Money exchange.

Men and women stumbled from the storefronts into the relative safety of the street. Some were wounded and bleeding. One or two were carried.

The troops left the Beetle in the pullout and scrambled on foot toward what was left of the buildings.

I drove slowly across the border into Mexico, forgetting all about entry papers and more concerned with where Caitrin was in the noise and blowing dust of the explosion.

The troops, distracted by the explosion, set off on foot to set up a perimeter around the damaged buildings. The Beetle pulled slowly out into the street. I halted to let it proceed in front of me. There'd be no vehicle pass for any of us now. I wasn't about to chance waiting any longer.

Caitrin must have driven past the explosion. I craned my neck from side to side as I searched cross-streets. I couldn't see the truck anywhere.

Fire trucks with sirens wailing—bomberos, according to the lettering on the side—approached the devastation from across the divided road. They turned in front of me and screeched to a halt.

My progress was blocked. I parked and ran past the fire trucks.

I had to find Caitrin.

I scanned the side streets, on the lookout for her truck. I walked back and detoured around the blocked street. I did a zig-zag of streets and alleys, searching on foot. Finally, I returned to the truck and headed slowly south on the way to Mexico 3.

I passed her in a corner of the empty bomberos fire hall parking lot.

Another bomberos scrambled out of the building, siren wailing.

I waited until it exited the lot. It had to be a miracle that Caitrin escaped the explosion. The last I saw, the truck looked to be engulfed in the flames.

I stopped in the middle of the road and honked.

She looked around and recognized me on the divided street. She waved frantically.

I did a U-turn to circle back.

She was panic-stricken. She jumped up and down and waved frantically even as I turned into the bomberos lot. Tears streamed down her face. She cast a glassy-eyed stare at me.

"Are you all right?" I asked her. "I thought I lost you. You disappeared after the explosion. I thought you were caught in it."

"I couldn't see you through the smoke and dust. I couldn't turn around. The policía blocked the streets. I didn't want to walk back in case there were more explosions." She halted, out of breath.

"It's all right. I found you. We can relax now," I said. "Did you see what happened?"

"It was a casa de cambio. A money exchange store. The explosion was huge. It looked like it might have taken out the entire block." She began trembling all over again. "I could have been in there exchanging money. I could have been killed."

"Caitrin, you're fine. We had a close call. We got lucky. The explosion missed us. We're learning as we go, and something we need to do right away is figure out what we're going to do to keep track of one another if something like this happens again."

"I tried calling on the radio. You wouldn't answer. In the mirror it looked like you were in the middle of the explosion," she explained.

Bits of glass were scattered on Caitrin's front and rear seats. "What happened to your windows? Were you that close?"

Small cuts on her right arm were bleeding. Trembling turned into violent shaking.

I led her to a bench in front of the fire station and sat her down before she fell down. "You were. Okay, we need to take a break. We'll park here until the trucks come back. I don't think it will be soon."

I walked back for the first aid kit. I swabbed the small cuts with alcohol and bandaged her arm. "You'll be as good as new in a day or two. Or three." I sat down beside her.

She reached for my hand and gripped it so hard I winced.

"I was worried. I couldn't find you anywhere. I thought your truck was caught in the explosion. The streets were blocked off. I couldn't turn around. I didn't know what to do. I couldn't go back. I could barely remember to check the radio."

It was my fault. I forgot to turn it on. She stood up and began pacing back and forth in front of me. "We just faced our first challenge. We didn't do very good, did we?"

We failed monumentally. If we couldn't keep track of one another, how long would we be able to survive in a new world while facing new challenges?

"Only two missing windows. We got lucky. I thought I lost you. I couldn't see you through the dust."

I wrapped my arms around her. "So much for money exchange. We'll have to wait until Ensenada. I don't want to spend any more time here than we have to."

It was an ordeal we escaped and survived to drive another day. We settled in the empty parking lot. I took out the remainder of our prepared food and we feasted as best we could with stomachs still nervous and upset from the explosion.

"If there's a gas station down the road, we'll pull in and try to pay with cash. Who knows, maybe they'll take our dollars at par or worse. I'll turn on my walkie-talkie. We'll figure it out as we go."

"I'm scared now, Russell. What if we get robbed?"

I was just as concerned. "We need to find a cantina. We need to sit and eat and take a break and talk. And you need to change. Keep your eyes open. I'll lead."

She hesitated. "What if we're doing the wrong thing? What if we should have stayed where we were? What if we do get robbed? What if the trucks get stolen?"

"Caitrin, we've come this far. We both had a shock. You especially. You were caught on the edge of the explosion. We'll stop and eat and talk and have a beer and figure out what we're going to do. I have the same concerns. You know that. But we have to keep moving. There's no reason for either of us to go back. Is there?

I was sure about me.

I wasn't so sure about Caitrin any more.

17

Risking it all

I came up on a roadside taquería and stopped. It would be as good a time as any to test our dollars.

Caitrin stopped behind me and got out.

"Woman, you look pretty good in those cutoffs. How did you manage and drive, too?"

She pretended to grab the hem of a skirt and curtsied while a grin pasted itself to her face. She knew how much I liked her long legs. "I have talents you haven't yet explored."

Even after all this time, I couldn't help but look her over. I looked her up and down and back up, unable to get enough of the woman. Her scarf still hid her breasts beneath the sheer blouse. I felt cheated. "Well, in that case, how about dishing out some of the dollars in your pack for tacos and beer? I'd treat you, but I don't have any money."

"Men. Always wanting something," she said, smiling.

"Women. You can't live with them—" I began. I didn't get a chance to finish.

"Don't you dare finish that sentence or I'll never wear another dress for you. Ever."

My hands reached for the sky. I held them up, as though surrendering. "I was going to say—"

"No, you weren't," she interrupted again. "Now let's eat."

She reached into her grab bag and handed over a fistful of dollars. "Wait. You wore that dress for me? I thought—"

"Hopefully, men will get women figured out in my lifetime." She mumbled something that sounded like Not before more than a few generations.

I took the dollars she offered and got out while the getting was still good. "Do you think they'll take them? What if they won't?"

I made for the taquería and returned with four tacos and a couple of Sol. Caitrin wasn't by our trucks.

Her scarf was in her back pocket and she was walking toward a man with a younger woman. They were standing by a beat-up old Beetle. It was parked ahead of us by a hundred feet or so.

It looked to be the same car that was pulled over at the border. The beater belched smoke as the woman behind the wheel stomped on the gas pedal again and again. The engine yielded to the torture and screamed its own form of obscenities.

Voices rose and fell in between the girl's attempts at keeping the engine running. Arms waved and fingers pointed and lips moved.

I was too far away to make anything out.

Caitrin looked over as I approached with the food.

She disengaged and rushed to meet me.

I was close enough to see the man's eyes appreciate her

departure as they looked her up and down. Her scarf was tucked into a pocket. Bouncing breasts and dark nipples bore down on me until she pulled the scarf out and tucked it into her shirt.

She didn't want me to meet the two she was talking with. She was being a little obvious with the scarf, too, almost as though I wasn't there. I gave up thinking about it when I got another look at her legs in the cutoffs.

"Mamasita gave me stink-eye, but she served up the food. Exchange is at par. No bargaining. She says we should be able to use dollars until we get to a bank. For now, at least."

Caitrin didn't appear to be relieved. "I'm still worried. That could change tomorrow. Or maybe even later today."

I considered lying to her. I decided against it and instead wolfed down the tacos and beer. We belched on our way back to the trucks.

"We're where we wanted to be," I said. "We planned it this way. We're going to have to suck it up and keep going. It won't be easy. We're in a new country with a different language. It'll take a while, but it will grow on us as long as we keep working together. I promise."

She nodded and turned her attention to the map. I pointed out the rest of Mexico 3. "The road to El Sauzal is two lanes. According to the scale, it's narrow and probably impossible to drive at night since we're not familiar with it."

"Are you that worried? What are we going to do?"

I couldn't tell her it wouldn't be dangerous. "It's around 75 miles, winding, narrow, with steep edges. Mexican drivers aren't the best on roads like those, so I've read."

"Are we going to keep on?" she asked.

"Yes. Until it gets close to dark. Then we're going to pull off before it gets pitch black and set up camp. For a change, we'll get a chance to sleep until daylight. I'm not driving on that road at night. I won't let you do it, either."

"What if we don't find somewhere to stop?" she asked.

I had already considered that. I didn't have an answer, but I tried. "In that case, we'll find a straight stretch, pull over as best we can, and wait. We'll put out markers and hope for an uneventful night."

It was the best I could come up with.

It turned out I was right about Mexico 3. It was a horrendous narrow, curving road, with hairpins that backtracked. Unpaved and uneven shoulders were steep and close to the sides, with little to no room for error. Oncoming vehicles careened around corners and took them wide. It was a struggle to make any set speed or distance.

We came up to a turnout visible on the side of a hill in the distance. I told her about it on the radio and waited. It crackled in silence. "What do you think? Do you want to keep going? Or would you rather we hold here until morning?"

Caitrin's voice quavered through the static over the radio. She had to be shaking like a leaf. It wasn't news to me she was unhappy with the driving conditions on this crazy road. "I want to stop."

I couldn't deny it. I wanted to stop, too. We could easily make Ensenada tomorrow. "I've had enough. Making my way through that explosion and not seeing you behind me scared me half to death. Driving this road has left me with nothing."

Our two-truck convoy pulled into the clearing hanging precipitously off the edge of a tall, rocky hill. Bushes high enough to hide behind stood out at the far end. I parked and got out. "Wait here. I'm going to see if there's room to park both vehicles."

Miraculously, no one had yet soiled the area behind the bushes with human waste. I whistled to get Caitrin's attention and motioned for her to park out of sight behind the bushes. I moved my own truck and trailer close in beside hers.

"We should probably string the proximity alarms," I said.

"If we do that, we might as well put up a tent. How about it, road captain?" she asked.

After our ordeal in the dark, we could use a nice sleep on an air mattress.

"I might even be talked into sharing your sleeping bag. Be sure you take out one big enough for two."

I dug out the tent and made sure I found the queen mattress. "You find the sleeping bags while I set this thing up."

In twenty minutes, we had the tent up and the air pump was working on the mattress. Caitrin searched through her vehicle. She held up a plastic bag with look of triumph when she found whatever it was she was looking for.

"What're you doing? What's in the bag?"

"Sheets," she said. "And you can't come in until I tell you it's all right."

I waited longer than I wanted. The air mattress squeaked and the sheets rustled. What could be taking the woman so long to make a bed? Considering how fast the two of us could unmake one, it shouldn't take so much time. "What are you doing in there?"

"You'll see in a minute. Be patient."

I killed more time with a quick wash and brushed my teeth. "I'm coming in, ready or not."

She mumbled something about being more than ready.

I unzipped the tent fly. She had made the bed and arranged the pillows. Caitrin waited beneath a sheet, arranged in a pose that promised a long and exhausting night. A grin pretty much said the cat was about to eat the canary.

"Well aren't you a sight for tired eyes."

She sighed. "You're still dressed. Let me help you with that."

Somehow, she managed to keep covered by the sheet while she unbuckled and unzipped. I was left with a pair of socks and a shirt. I made short work of the shirt by ripping it open and tossing it in a corner.

I didn't bother with the socks.

Neither of us wanted to waste the time.

Caitrin called out as our fevered love-making took her over the edge again and again. She hadn't been this fervent and eager since our first few times together.

Exhausted bodies separated. The sheet fell away.

Caitrin's scarf was tied over her breasts like a tube top.

We slept well but for the few times the alarm sounded. It woke us, but we were well-hidden. Lacking vehicle noise and without people on the road, it had to be animals. Once we got onto the main road to

Ensenada, I was sure we would encounter a lot more vehicles and people.

Our voyage would begin in earnest.

We had crossed the border to relative safety and discovered more people in the same situation we found ourselves to be in. The locals were friendly toward us. We knew nothing about the bomb blast in Tecate. That was a hazard of not being able to speak the language, but we could do nothing about that for now.

"Who was that couple you were talking to yesterday?" Caitrin shifted her gaze and busied herself adjusting the sheets. "Just two people in the same boat. They were the couple in front of us arguing with the border guard. Todd's a nice guy, but his girlfriend can be a bit of a bitch, apparently."

I let it go, not wanting to be burdened by people I didn't know. I had enough on my plate. We had enough on both our plates.

"It's warm in here, wouldn't you say?" I pulled the covers off. Caitrin was naked beneath. I kissed my way from breast to breast. She sighed and pulled me closer.

"Do we have time?" Caitrin slipped down to rest her head on my stomach.

I didn't want to be a spoilsport, but we had places to be, even if we were safe across the border. "Not if we make out like we did last night. You were an animal."

She pretended to punch me in the stomach.

"I was not. Even if I was. So what?"

I grinned so hard I thought my face would never be right. "You don't need to get all defensive on me. I was there right along with you, remember?"

"So that was you? I couldn't tell in the dark. I thought maybe—"

I decided to quit while I was ahead. "You were amazing. And noisy, too."

"That was me? I thought it was you."

She finished me with her mouth and climbed off the bed. It seemed as though she took her sweet time dressing with a purpose in mind.

"I think we need more of the same later today, wouldn't you say?" I asked.

She dropped her blouse. "How much later did you have in mind?"

"Cover up, sweetheart. It's not good to fool with mother nature," I teased.

"Speaking of which, did you remember to pack my pills? They were in that box by the kitchen table."

18

Russell

A downhill straight stretch of road forced our heavy vehicles and their overheated brakes to slow and finally stop to allow them time to cool. In the distance, at the bottom, just before a shallow curve, a car was off the road in the ditch.

"We'll stop for them as soon as our brakes cool. Does that look like that Beetle? It must be Todd."

Caitrin brightened at the mention of his name. "Maybe it is. I don't think he's getting along with his partner."

We advanced and I slowed precipitously as the curve came up. I put down the window to offer help. I couldn't get a word in.

The couple in the Beetle from the taco stand were loud in their disagreement over Todd's driving. The woman's shrill voice cast the blame onto her partner.

Of course, if he was driving. I heard him admit as much.

"Can we help?"

It was only then that Todd looked back down the road to see Caitrin approaching on foot. He smiled and waved. "We've run off the road. I think it's the brakes."

"Or your stupid driving. Why wouldn't you listen? I told you the brakes were mushy yesterday," Jessica said.

"Blah blah blah. Hi Caitrin. I wondered if you would show up."

Caitrin smiled back. "Just in time, by the look of it. What's up, Todd?"

Jessica turned to Caitrin "This useful idiot wouldn't believe me when I told him the brakes wouldn't be able to handle the hill. Thus, we are in the ditch and otherwise failing to proceed." She looked back at Todd and rolled her eyes.

"Shut up, woman. I did the best I could."

She scowled back. Her hands rested against shapely hips. Todd was almost as lucky as I was. "Your best isn't good enough judging by where you parked. It's a ditch, in case you can't tell."

She smiled at Caitrin and appeared to be assessing her mechanical abilities. She ignored me until she couldn't any longer. I think she gave in because she didn't think Caitrin would be capable of assisting. "Do you think you could help us?"

I dug around in the trailer for my tool box while Caitrin consoled the couple with an explanation of hills and brakes and old cars.

"You see, Todd? Even she knows when to take it easy," Jessica said. "Why couldn't you?"

"Maybe because you were doing the telling, Jess. As usual," Todd complained.

The woman abandoned Todd and Caitrin and came to stand beside me at the back of my truck. I lifted the small toolbox out of the trailer. She offered to carry it to the disabled Beetle.

"Thanks, Jess. Just put it anywhere by your car. I'll be over in a minute."

"You're welcome. And it's not Jess. It's Jessica."

"Good to know, Jessica. I'll be right with you."

I shifted things around until I found a container of brake fluid. It could be a loose fitting that needed tightening. A bit of brake fluid would top off the loss. "If we're lucky, Jessica, it'll be an easy fix. If not—" I hesitated.

"If not?" she asked.

"It'll take us a little longer, is all. Everything will be fine. I noticed you gunning the engine at the taco stand. Judging by the cloud coming out of the exhaust, I'd say you're burning oil. I'll check the level for you, too, if it's all right."

I got down on the ground and eased myself under their vehicle. Brake fluid dripped from a fitting. I put a small adjustable on it and gently tightened the brake line fitting. The line was crimped in the middle where a rock hit it. Or a rock they ran over.

I eased out from beneath the car. I was greeted by Jessica's long legs ending in cutoffs. The tall girl's legs were longer than Caitrin's by a mile. I looked up at her and smiled.

By the look on her face, she knew I was squinting through the sun to do it.

"It's a brake line. I've—" I started to explain. She didn't let me finish.

"Is it serious? Will I be able to keep going?"

"I've got some hose clamps and a bit of rubber line that should fit. As long as you don't do any more desert racing, you'll be fine.

I went back to the truck to retrieve the hose and clamps. When I returned, Jessica was waiting beneath the Beetle.

I crawled in beside her.

"See there?" I rubbed a finger on it. "It's a hole."

She closed her fingers on it. "Oh. Yeah. I can feel it. It's rough."

I cut a break in the line and smoothed the ends. Jessica helped hold the metal line steady. I tried to keep our conversation light.

Caitrin and Todd were murmuring and deep in conversation out of sight behind our trucks.

"You must have driven over some rocks or a stray cactus or something."

"I'd like to drive over Todd's head."

I chuckled softly. "I hear you. Unfortunately, I can't help with that."

Jessica's smaller hands helped me get the patch hose over the frayed line. I tightened a clamp and allowed her to tighten the second. To be sure, I checked her work. "There. All done. See how easy it was? You're a good mechanic."

I handed her the rag before taking it back to clean my hands.

I crawled from beneath the car and opened the engine cover and checked the oil. "I've got a couple of quarts I can lend you. Do you know where to add it?"

She nodded and unscrewed the cap.

She took the quart, added all of it, and checked the stick. "Good to go. Thank you, Mr. Good Samaritan. I don't know what I'd do without you. Now where did that asshole get to? He's probably trying to make time with your partner."

Jessica turned to the trucks. "Todd. Quit flirting and get your ass over here. It's time to get back on the road."

Already late because of the brake repair on Todd's VW, we settled in for the next fifty miles and hustled to make Ensenada by late afternoon on the narrow, treacherous road. I encouraged Caitrin on the two-way radio, and she seemed a lot calmer on this part of the highway. With two loaded half-ton trucks towing two heavily-laden trailers, it was all we could do to make forty miles an hour. Much of the time, we were slowed to thirty.

We stopped for fuel and tacos before heading into downtown Ensenada. We couldn't avoid it. The main highway went right through the center of town. She called me on the radio. "Is that Todd's car?"

The faded white Beetle was parked half on the sidewalk. It must have struggled into Ensenada in front of us. Todd and his girlfriend were nowhere to be seen. "It's probably one that looks the same. They all look alike down here."

The radio crackled. "What did you say her name was?" I asked.

"I never said," Caitrin replied. "I don't know her name."

I knew. It was Jessica. Caitrin appeared to be familiar enough with Todd.

Ensenada had a definite party atmosphere going on. Crowds of drunken revelers, most of them gringos like us, wandered from one side of the street to the other. Some stopped to puke or urinate in alleys. Some yelled greetings and waved as we stopped on the side of the street.

We pulled over in the middle of all of this. Neither of us was sure it was the right thing. "What are we going to do with the trucks? We can't leave them. We need a campsite so we can keep watch."

Caitrin opened up the map. A finger traced a route south from downtown Ensenada. She pulled out one of the guide books stashed in the glove box and flipped it open to a dog-eared page. "Santo Tomás. It's thirty miles. According to the book, it has a couple of wineries. Maybe we could camp out on the edge of one. It has to be safer than staying in downtown Ensenada. If we stay here, our trucks will end up getting looted."

In the mirror's reflection, I saw Caitrin craning her neck as she passed the Beetle. Her head swiveled from side to side, obviously on the lookout for the couple. She stared straight ahead for the rest of the drive through town, never once casting a glance away from the road.

Maybe it was from all our nighttime driving.

In an hour we were in tiny Santo Tomás. It was barely more than a blip by the side of the highway. A bar and a restaurant had enough room to park a few vehicles. A hotel overlooked the highway on top of a low cliff. The sign advertised eighteen-dollar rooms, and I wondered how outdated the price was, given the fading letters.

Past a Pemex, I drove across Mexico 1 to the shady edge of a campground. A light breeze circulated past the trees and helped cool the shade. Rustling branches and leaves contributed to our disconnect from the many dangerous miles we'd piled up over the past few days.

A huge black SUV stopped at the restaurant we only just passed. Doors opened and two people stepped out. A couple that looked suspiciously like Todd and the girl from the broke-down Beetle unloaded their ever-increasing pile of belongings. They ended up carrying it across the highway to settle in a couple of hundred feet from us.

"There's that couple," Caitrin said. "I'm going to go and introduce myself again. It looks like they might have lost their car. Maybe they can travel with us."

I didn't try to dissuade Caitrin. I knew better.

"I'll get started putting up the tent."

Caitrin returned, happy at seeing familiar faces in the same pickle as we were in. I was busy struggling with the tent poles.

"You're having trouble getting it up, aren't you? I can help with that."

She got down on her hands and knees and crawled inside. She pushed the flaps aside to reveal herself leaning back on her elbows. Exposed breasts and a come-hither look said I should come hither.

"They don't have very much money," she said. "They're almost broke. Todd says just about everyone who came down here arrived after all the banks were closed."

I slipped inside. Eager hands fumbled to unzip. "Where are they from?"

Caitrin reached into my jeans. "San Diego. Todd's an airman. The woman is his girlfriend, I think. Todd and Jessica. Or maybe they just hooked up. I'm not sure."

"We need to be careful, Caitrin. We're traveling with all this stuff. A lot of people didn't come with anything. What happened with their car?"

"Oh, I think it broke down. I told Todd they could

ride with us," Caitrin said.

I shook my head, unbelieving.

She finished with me and tucked me back inside before changing into a bra and buttoning her blouse.

"Caitrin—"

"Did I do a bad thing?"

"I don't know. We'll find out for sure when they rob us, I guess," I said.

She rushed off to pass along the good news. She didn't appear concerned. Perhaps she was a better Samaritan that I could ever be.

Todd and Jessica showed up as we were sitting down to eat. They were all grins and funny stories about their trip in a beater that finally gave out a few miles north of Santo Tomás. There was something about that, though. I couldn't remember any vehicles broke down by the side of the road.

"I turned off the main road to go down this sand path," Todd explained. "I thought the beach might be nearby. The engine must have seized. There was no oil on the dipstick."

I started to think Todd was the only dipstick within sight, but I only sighed and looked across the table. Jessica pointedly ignored me and busied herself tucking a napkin in and spreading it over her shirt."

Two more plates came out thanks to Caitrin and we shared our meager rations, such as they were. I didn't get so much as a thank you. Caitrin didn't notice. She was too busy paying attention to Todd's tale of misery and woe interspersed with attempts at humor.

I paid close cattention to the details of his story. Parts of it at least appeared to be true. Their car had been the one in front of us at the border, waiting to cross. And we'd crossed paths with it again on Mexico 3—or Caitrin had, at least.

Then came the brake failure at the bottom of the hill, where I'd repaired it with Jessica's help. She turned out to be more useful than Todd. I looked over at their campsite. All of their belongings appeared to be parked outside their tent, without even so much as a cover.

Caitrin was at ease in Todd's company. A friendship was developing between them. She laughed at his jokes, sometimes giggling in appreciation. The wine came out. It would be a long night.

I left the festivities early to climb into the tent. Caitrin and Todd and Jessica must have emptied the box of wine.

The last thing I remember before falling asleep was Jessica saying good night. The conversation became more subdued between Todd and Caitrin. Eventually, it quieted to whispers and I fell asleep.

I had no idea how late it was when Caitrin finally came to bed. I turned on the light. "What happened?"

She quickly turned her back and removed her blouse. The bra she put on when she dressed in front of me was missing. There wasn't a mark left behind.

"What do you mean?" she asked.

"The front of your shirt is all wet."

"It's nothing. I spilled something on it."

Whatever it was, it wasn't red wine.

The sheets rustled as Caitrin slipped out of bed and rushed to dress. She rummaged through her bag, and then closed the snaps and pulled the drawstrings. I opened my eyes and caught her standing over me, staring down. "You're up early. What's up?"

"I made a decision last night. I'm leaving. Todd has agreed to come with me."

I sat up, unsure how to respond. In truth, I wasn't surprised. Last night's activities sealed it for me. I hated to admit that I wondered what she was doing hooking up with me after her relationship with Konnor fell apart. Perhaps it was more than what she told of his madness and the supposed beatings he inflicted on her.

"What about Jessica?" I asked. She was turning into a third wheel.

"He hasn't told her anything. She's in the store across the street."

Of course he hadn't told the woman anything. The man didn't have any balls, other than the come he deposited on Caitrin's shirt last night. I knew now that Caitrin was a creature of opportunity. When she felt the one she was with no longer had anything to offer, she went in search of a fresh partner. Well, good luck with that when the only thing recommending the change was a missing bra, oral sex and a stained blouse.

"I can't hold you back. But I have a question for you, and you're not going to like it."

She undid the tent fly and got down on all fours to crawl out.

"Did you tell Todd about your gold?" I asked.

She ignored me and dragged her pack out of the tent. Two doors on her truck slammed. She drove out onto the highway, headed south. She didn't bother to wave good-bye.

I dressed and went looking for Jessica. I found her in the small store.

She didn't seem upset that Todd pulled up stakes with Caitrin in her truck. "Too bad about your woman. She's in for a shock once she gets to know that one for sure."

I asked about Todd, but she didn't know a lot. She'd picked him up by the side of the road with his thumb stuck out. As soon as her car broke down on the dirt road, he turned ice cold and pretty much ignored her until we arrived. I guess he knew he had another live one when he spotted too-friendly Caitrin.

It was unfortunate. Together, we'd worked hard to get ready for this trip. We committed time and effort and planning, and now it was all for nothing. I enjoyed Caitrin's company on our trek, though. Now I wondered if I could entice Jessica to sign up.

"You want a ride?" Jessica was younger, but not by much. Maybe five years. A lot taller, though. I'd checked out her long legs when she helped me with her broke-down Beetle. Those legs would be good for walking if we ever found a place to stay and explore. And here I was, already thinking of her as a life partner.

I never learned.

"Sure. I'll ride along. No strings, though. I'm free as a bird and I want to stay that way."

I smiled across at her. "In that case, you're probably happy to be rid of Todd, aren't you?"

She didn't answer. She looked out the window, instead.

"That's all right. I'm happy to be rid of him, too," I told her.

"What about Caitrin? Are you happy she's gone?" Jessica asked.

"I didn't realize she was so fickle. So maybe. But I can't force someone to stay who doesn't want to."

"I like the way you think." Jessica put the seatback down, sighed, and closed her eyes. "I haven't been in a bed this comfortable in quite a while. Wake me when you get somewhere."

I was happy to be almost alone with my thoughts.

Caitrin had to have told Todd about the gold. Or maybe she only hinted at it. No matter. Todd read her like a book. I couldn't fault the man for climbing aboard.

There was one other thought. Perhaps Caitrin and Todd had been partners all along during the many months we'd been preparing for our trip.

I pressed the pedal just a little farther to the floor and hoped I wouldn't be too late.

19

Beyond la frontera

It **didn't take long** for two more expat gringos to get into the party atmosphere going on wherever they congregated. Jessica was pretty easy-going. She enjoyed joking around, and often made light of the seriousness of our situation. She never joked about my choice of Caitrin, though.

Jessica made plain during those occasions when Caitrin's name came up that it was quite clear Caitrin was the one responsible for our meeting. I couldn't dispute that. I was happy with the situation I found myself in with Jessica.

When it came to the more serious things such as the suitability of campsites and weather patterns associated with time of year, she was without equal. She had a background in meteorology. Climbing was a hobby. She could hike for miles non-stop. No wonder she was so eager to leave her car behind and not pay good money she didn't have to get it repaired.

That, and I came along, suddenly single and solo with

a truck and a trailer. She teased me about that, too, and I'd smile and laugh and pretend to ignore her. It still hurt, though, that Caitrin, the woman that helped me get prepared for this trip, deserted me for lack of a bra, a messy, stained shirt, and a stranger.

I told the not so funny story to Jessica. She laughed it off. In the end, I figured she was the one with the good attitude about it. "Men. You can't live with them, and you can't kill them."

"Excuse me, but I think that's my line about women," I insisted.

"In that case, oh savior of mine, we've got us a Mexican standoff."

I'd ever heard it put that way before. Not so obvious, at least. One thing I refused to do was mention the cash I carried along with the firearms in the secret compartment beneath the bed of our half-ton. I never told Caitrin about the cash, either, which was why it was still there.

I figured it could only bring more grief than I needed after Caitrin's hasty departure.

Jessica and I spent a lot of time talking about what went on back home during the time before we left. I learned she did almost exactly the same things I had.

She moved out to the burbs while trying to keep a low profile. She stocked up on reserves of food and water. She hadn't managed to find a house with underground water storage. It impressed her I thought of it, and even more that I found one.

She too had a generator and small hot water heaters and an electric bicycle she kept charged with solar panels. She never considered having anything to do with picking up a new truck for her trek south. And she never thought of checking for AM radio stations.

She managed to get tangled up with one or two men. When things got out of hand, and they locked her out, she chucked them to the winds and moved on. It meant starting over with everything. It was right around then she discovered the men in her life needed her more than she needed them.

She made sure to avoid further encumbrances until she found herself tangled up with Todd. She didn't have to elaborate further. I saw enough with his antics at the border, and with Caitrin.

The only reason Jessica headed south to the Baja was because she and her girlfriends often come down to party long before the troubles began. It was a familiar place to watch the desert races and raise hell in the bars and street parties.

"So then. Get drunk. Get laid. Get your hungover ass home." I grinned, not expecting a response.

"Exactly. You get the idea."

At least the woman was honest about it. I gave her props for that.

In our travels, we tried to keep a low profile. We stopped often, always on the lookout for isolated, semi-permanent camping sites. We'd smile and acknowledge the friendlier locals, often engaging them in our stilted gringo Spanish. We ended up smiling and nodding a lot, as did they.

Our local travel was limited to getting fresh vegetables and replacement for goods with expired best before dates, or small things that I forgot or decided not to bring at the last minute. I picked up items for Jessica, too. I wanted her to feel like she was a part of things, even if she eventually ended up moving on.

No way did we want to draw attention to ourselves,

unlike the hundreds of others that partied it up, 24/7. It didn't take long before the authorities demanded their pound of flesh for allowing people such as us to remain where we camped.

Bribes—mordida, in Spanish—were demanded and paid. It became rampant after only a couple of months.

Our home was our vehicle and wherever we decided to park. It didn't help when many of the revelers showed a certain amount of curiosity that turned into jealousy at the truck and trailer we commanded. Wandering eyes took in the loads of equipment on board. That we were organized seemed to aggravate them, to some extent.

It got so bad we stopped going to evening bonfires. Eventually, we ran out of excuses. We'd arrive at a new spot, stay a couple of days until the intrusions and the questioning became persistent, and then we'd move on. We did that in the dark of night.

The more dedicated preppers would hang around for a day or two, as we did, and they too would move on. We noticed the numbers of on-site campers diminish radically. It looked as though we would be among the last of the die-hard survivalists to leave these groups, never to return.

Those remaining would be partiers and hangers-on intent on capitalizing on the booze, drugs and the women who used them for it. We took ourselves and our gear farther south, distant from the border and the protection it might afford if we ever needed to return home.

We weren't looking for much. We wanted a place to stop and live, full time if we could find one. We had everything we needed to set up a permanent camp. All we needed was a location that was suitable, isolated, and far from the crowd of adventurers that, like us, made good their escape and were looking for much the same.

Perhaps our expectations were too high, although neither Jessica nor I thought so. In any case, it didn't really matter.

We packed up and prepared to leave our very last gathering of expats. We didn't bother saying goodbye. Any acquaintances we had made were at best transient. Too many questions would follow. We wanted to lay low and leave without making waves.

At first light, we headed off under blue sky and a rising sun we knew would only grow hotter as the day progressed. Down the road, we pulled over and set up the solar panels to charge the batteries our equipment needed to operate. It was a simple task to hook up the color-coded leads to charge radios, laptops, cell phones, walkie-talkies and standby batteries

At least we had that routine down pat. Neither of us had ever been this deep into Mexico before, and only Jessica had ever been on the Baja peninsula. This experience, like every other that occurred in our brief lives, was brand new.

By nightfall, analog radio stations from Central America began to skip off the ionosphere. We tried tuning in different English broadcasts to catch up on the latest news around the world. To say we were shocked by what we heard would be an understatement.

There were rumors of a virus flareup in the Far East. It was spreading far and wide around the world thanks to airplanes and cruise ships. A British doctor that caught the airborne disease had become ill and supposedly been cured with a new drug. He flew home and infected everyone on the airplane, as well as those who passed through the airport terminal with him.

We found it strange that we never heard any of this when we were at home. Even if we had, it would have been labeled as fake news. Apparently, there was a lot of that going around.

So much for modern medicine. It began to get depressing, and we decided to listen in only two nights a week. Then, after a couple more weeks, we ceased caring entirely.

What we heard wasn't good for our mental health.

We didn't talk about it right away. We had camp to set up, a tent to erect and food to prepare. If it was dark, we did our set-up under the glare of the headlights and then went to blackout. There was no sense in alerting anyone passing by that we were off in the distance and away from the main highway.

Once we settled in for the evening, our fears came to the surface, thanks to the two different news broadcasts we heard. This time, there would be very little chance of escaping the coming craziness we knew would overtake the country we so eagerly adopted.

It wasn't as though we were expecting much. All we wanted was to stop roaming like vagrants, even if we were better equipped. A place to call home on a permanent basis would be nice. We moved so many times we felt like gypsies. And perhaps we were, even now, for we were still on the move.

If only we could find a spot that was isolated and offered shelter. It had to be out of sight of a roadway. It had to have fresh running water. When that happened, we were equipped to remain forever if we wanted.

That was our dream, at least.

"We'll double our efforts tomorrow. Perhaps if we followed some of the off-road trails we'd be more successful."

"I'll follow you anywhere, Russell. You know that, right?"

I looked across the seat at Jessica and smiled. It was easy. She was turning out to be a real asset. "Yes. I know that now. I hope you know how much of an asset you are. The trails will be slow going in a loaded truck. It will be more rewarding if we can find a permanent spot to settle down.

I was reluctant to use the word home. I didn't want to let on that the trailer would make it impossible for us to pursue many of the more isolated trails that Jessica wanted us to explore.

I was deep into worry and even more confused by the news we listened to earlier. The shit was hitting the fan. If we weren't careful, it would be scattered over both of us whether we wanted it or not.

Would it never end?

Jessica and I only just made good our separate escapes from a country that so isolated itself from its people and its neighbors as to be non-existent. Neither of us could figure out why the government did such a thing. We gave up trying. We no longer considered it to be our country or our home.

By accident we discovered Mexico, with its analog radio stations and friendly people, was a godsend. And thanks to the speed with which Jessica picked up Spanish, we remained on good terms with the locals.

There were others like us who recognized they too

needed to escape from the madness to the north. The trouble was, though, that the madness had ended, and not in a good way. The country, as far as we could tell, was empty except for the military patrols, and the few who remained behind.

What was going on was anyone's guess. Perhaps it was the one percent that the media so adored that remained behind in a country empty of everything but madness.

What that one percent consisted of, neither Jessica nor I knew. We didn't want to know. We were just happy to be here.

That's why the reports of the virus outbreak in the Far East set our alarm bells sounding once again. The efforts at containment appeared doomed to fail, given what news reports were saying.

Rioting citizens, quarantines, and border closings by terrified governments, faked reports of drug cures, and medical doctors and evangelists praising God's miraculous cures all contributed to the scaremongering.

Yet again, what occurred in our own country was being perpetrated on another continent, although by a different scare entirely.

Across the Atlantic, it was about the virus.

A trip to a library cleared it up.

The virus apparently originated in a food market. Symptoms occurred anywhere from five to seven days after being in contact with a carrier. It was airborne. If you were unhealthy, you were more likely to catch it and spread it, given the incubation time. The virus had no treatment.

And then the silliness started.

Masks were good. Masks were no good. And on and on it went. Protests. Riots. Shortages of food and dry goods. The stupidity and silliness were only beginning. Of course, we didn't know that. It was all labeled fake news by then.

It was most likely headed this way. It had been held off only as long as it had because Mexico kept its international airports closed.

We slept on this new information for a couple of days. Jessica put away the blanket she used to separate sides in the tent. We shared a bed for an agreed-upon week.

Jessica turned out to be an enthusiastic lover. By the end of the week, I hoped she'd want to make it permanent. When she did, I was relieved. We eagerly accepted that we'd make it permanent—or at least for what passed as permanent these days.

She seemed happy. We'd taken our time and gotten to know one another first. When it happened, it was only right. It was enjoyable for both of us, too, I think.

Jessica was warm and inviting. Often, we clung to one another and remained awake to talk, long after our bouts of fevered, sweaty love-making. That she had the longest legs on any woman I'd ever known didn't hurt, and she knew it.

I made sure she caught me looking every time. She didn't seem to mind. In fact, I was pretty certain she was encouraging me with the shorts and the sheer shirts and the filmy skirts and dresses she seemed to have in endless supply.

We stopped in Loreto for fuel and a quick feed of tacos. Jessica loved those things almost as much as

I did. We ate our fill, picked up a sixer of beer, and stashed it in a cooler.

We took a quick tour of the malecón on foot and wandered hand in hand back to our truck. Before long, we found ourselves off the main road on a turnout, sharing a beer. Below us, a sand beach and the vast expanse of the Golfo de California presented itself.

"What do you think?" I asked her.

The steep, rocky trail leading down the side of the hill concerned me. While it appeared to be unused, there definitely had to be a reason for it to exist. I casually wandered over for a better look. I climbed over the barrier and struggled to walk down twenty or thirty feet.

It just might be wide enough for truck and trailer.

"If we have to climb out of there with the trailer, the truck might not be capable of pulling it. I'd like to hike down for a better look." I was concerned for Jessica's safety. And my own if she got hurt.

"I'll worry about you doing it alone," she said.

Now that I found a good woman, the prospect of losing this one was too much for me to contemplate. Still, I gave her free rein to do the job.

"You should go. You're the climbing expert. I've coasted down steeper territory than this only in my dreams. You need to know I'll be worried until you get back up the hill."

Jessica loaded her backpack with water and energy bars while I made sandwiches. She threw a loop of hiking rope cross-ways over her shoulder.

"You'd better not be asleep and dreaming when you drive our truck down the side of that hill. If you get hurt, I'll kill you."

"No, you won't. You'll nurse me back to health

because I think I might love you." That admission ought to hold her for a while.

Jessica stuck out her tongue as she climbed over the barrier. "Me too. I'll see you on the flip side."

"Wait." I handed over a radio. "If it looks good, say the word. I'll be listening. We'll save a lot of time if you don't have to climb back up."

"That's what I like about you. You're always thinking. I'll be waiting at the bottom if you don't roll it up into a ball. I'll also be naked and eager and squeaky clean from a swim in the Golfo."

That picture pretty much sealed the deal for me. "Promises, promises. You know just what to say to the boys, don't you?"

"I know what to say to my boy."

I put my hands in my pockets, shrugged my shoulders, and kicked up dirt.

"Remember. If you end up rolling it up into a ball, I'll still be naked and squeaky clean, but I'll be running away from the wreck of Russell."

Jessica took her toothy grin with her as she disappeared down the hill.

I shook my head.

Women.

20

Paradise found

I reached for the radio half a dozen times in the ten minutes it took Jessica to check in. I pretended a certain level of nonchalance with my reply, although I was ecstatic to finally hear her voice.

"I've covered about a third of the distance. It's very narrow. Rough. Steep. The ground is solid, though. Traction will probably be good. I'll call again in a bit."

"Let me know when you get your clothes off, my little Golfo sea urchin."

"Aww."

Passing traffic was limited to semis and the occasional car or half-ton. When I remembered to check, almost all the cars and light trucks appeared to have Baja plates.

I sat back in the truck, door open, water bottle in hand, worrying. Who would see the truck and trailer? Who would bother to pay attention? Who would stop, wondering if I needed help? Would I be capable of telling a lie with a straight face and insist I was only taking a break before driving on?

A carload of gringos roared past, music blaring. They screeched to a stop past the turnout, backed up, and pulled in beside me.

"Russell! Where ya been, man? How's it going? Where's the little hottie you were with? Did she pack up and leave?"

Shit. They recognized me from when Caitrin and I were together. They were drunk or stoned or both, judging by the cans they tossed and the cloud of smoke that escaped open windows.

"I've been around. Where you off to?"

"We heard about a place farther south, near the border somewhere. We're on our way to check it out."

The Baja was two states, norte and sur. They had to be talking about the border to Baja sur. "Yeah, I heard about that place too." I lied, but they'd never know. Hell, they were stoned out of their minds. "Maybe I'll see you there in a day or two," I added. Another lie. I was getting good.

"Great. Okay. Say, you got anything we can snack on? We ran out about twenty miles north."

If they had any sense of where they were, they could have picked up more in Loreto.

"Loreto? Where's that?"

They missed the signs and the turnoff. Too stoned, probably. "Sure. Give me a minute." I dug in the back seat and came up with a couple of tinfoil bags and some jerky."

"Thanks, man. See you in paradise.

I nodded.

A female voice giggled, accompanied by the sound of bags being torn open. Doors slammed. Someone handed me a beer out an open window. "Here ya go. Enjoy." The car backed up. Wheels spun. Tires screeched on asphalt.

The beer was warm. They didn't even have the sense

to buy a cooler. Perhaps with the crowded back seat, there was no room. I popped the top and tipped it in their direction. "Thanks. I'll be sure to look you up," I called.

When the Baja freezes over.

I poured the warm beer on the ground.

The radio crackled. Jessica's call came through exactly forty-seven minutes into her hike. Not that I was counting the minutes, or anything.

"I would have called sooner, but I was busy taking off my clothes and going for a swim. The truck can make it. Just be careful. If you're not—" The transmission halted.

"I know. I know. You'll be naked and running for the hills," I reminded both of us.

It took longer than I thought to jockey the truck and trailer into position. Even then, I set the brake and got out to look a final time before committing to what could end up a disaster. The downslope appeared even steeper. Still rocky. Still a mule trail just wide enough if I took it slow. Real slow.

I said a silent prayer. Brakes, don't fail me now.

I guided the two-wheel-drive truck carefully, riding the brakes all the way. It definitely wasn't built for this. It wasn't a road. It resembled a dirt bike trail.

The truck groaned and rocked side to side. The brakes squealed and the trailer skipped back and forth like it wanted to pass me. I fought the steering wheel's attempts to spin out of control.

Half-way down I halted and called Jessica. "I'm really uncomfortable with this trailer behind me. It's causing problems."

I got out and walked partway down and back to the

truck. It was doable. If I went slow. "I'll see you at the bottom," I radioed.

"I'm waiting like a puppy that wants her tummy scratched."

If Jessica was thinking that would get me to take my time, she was sadly misinformed. A cloud of dust enveloped the truck and trailer as it bounced the rest of the way down the hill. I fought for control anyway, notwithstanding the picture of a naked Jessica waiting for me.

True to her word, Jessica, naked and wet from her swim in the Golfo, awaited. She had a huge grin on her face.

I couldn't be sure, but the grin I had might have been just a bit bigger.

She wouldn't let me out of the truck. Instead, she forced me to follow her long legs and firm, perfect tush. She kept looking back, allowing me to see her naked front, too.

Just when I began thinking she was teasing me, she directed me to a small rock face hidden from above by an overhang. Our truck and trailer would be completely obscured from anyone at the top of the hill.

I circled the wagons and parked.

After stripping down, I picked Jessica up and carried her into the Golfo. We laughed and splashed and swam and made wet, salty, sandy love on a beach blanket by the truck.

"What was it you mumbled just before I climbed over the barricade? I couldn't hear you properly."

We were pulling on clothes against the cool air.

"What? That? It was nothing." I grinned so hard I couldn't close my eyes. "So you did hear me."

"Well, I can't be a hundred percent certain. Why don't you tell me again?"

"I love you, too." Ever the practical one, I had one last thing that needed to get done. "Before we let it go to our heads, we need to brush out the tire tracks. We can use those dead palm fronds on the ground."

Maybe I wasn't so practical after all. We tore off our clothes and made love one more time. When we finished, it was dark enough to start in on covering our tracks down the hill.

"Be careful. The edges on the stem are sharp as hell."

We put on gloves, gathered multiple sharp-edged fronds, and brushed. We made out the occasional set of headlights above us as cars and heavy trucks went by. None halted at the turnout.

"Tomorrow we'll build a palapa just like the ones we saw earlier. All we'll be missing is the cement floor."

"I did a bit of exploring while I waited for you. There's a trickle of water coming off the cliff behind us. It's fresh. And filtered by the rock and sand."

We didn't bother setting up the tent. In the dark we spiked the corners and crawled inside. We fell into a happy and exhausted sleep in each other's arms with the tent all around us.

What else could we do now that we were home?

On day one, we celebrated by forgoing clothing. Instead, we pulled on our gloves and wove palm fronds into a roof for our palapa. Sharp spikes scratched and cut into our skin. We finished by setting up the tent beneath it.

The palapa provided perfect shade, even if the

support was only temporary. Once we settled in, we'd be able to pick up lumber in Loreto to make a more permanent roof.

It was as though we were our own private nudist colony of two on the beach. We romped naked, swam and explored and made love and eventually found the time to complete our camp setup. We weren't in a rush. There was nothing else we had to do.

We climbed into the tent and slept and made love and went back to sleep in a tangle of exhausted, sweaty legs and arms. It was almost like a honeymoon. By dark of our second day, we shared our relief at finally finding a home we could be proud of.

"Tomorrow we can launch the kayak and throw out a line to see what we come up with. If we can fish, we're almost home-free."

"Yeah. All you have to do is catch one."

I thumped my chest. "Man catch fish. Woman clean fish. Woman cook fish. Man eat fish. Woman prepare for sex."

"I think you're leaving out a couple of steps, but for now I'll let you live your fantasy. If things get out of hand, I'll be the one with the sharp knife cleaning fish and doing dishes, apparently."

We laughed and made long, slow, lazy love again.

Days turned into weeks. I went out fishing every other day, usually just before dawn to minimize the chance of being seen. Sometimes Jess went. Sometimes, we both went. We caught as many as we needed. We made one, sometimes two trips into town a month in the kayak, mostly for staples.

Sometimes we'd detour over the water and paddle a mile or two along the beach. We'd bring a blanket and sandwiches and have a picnic to make uninhibited love under the rising sun over the Golfo.

Our idyllic lifestyle hid the real reason we were here. We left behind our own country for reasons that never became clear. We knew something had gone wrong. We had no idea what it was, or whether there was anyone left to investigate and solve the crisis—or whether there was even an actual crisis.

I lost count of how many months we had been a couple when Jessica dropped the bombshell following a particularly enthusiastic and enjoyable night of celebration and love-making.

"I think I might be pregnant."

I swallowed hard and sat up in the tent. She already knew what I was going to ask.

"About six weeks, give or take. I didn't start counting until, you know, I missed my period."

"That's amazing. We have to get you to a doctor. We have to make sure everything is all right. We have to make sure you get proper food and rest and and—"

She pulled me down beside her. "Can we do that? What if someone—"

I wouldn't allow her to finish. "That's exactly why we have to visit a doctor. We have to find out."

"It'll expose us to the rest of the world when I check into a doctor's office for a pregnancy test. Even going to emerg could cause us problems. We have no health care, nothing."

I liked the way she used we, too. "We wouldn't have any back home, either. I read somewhere it's cheap down here. We could claim to be refugees or something. Maybe that would make it go better."

"I don't want to think about it now. Let's take the kayak out for a paddle."

We pulled ashore at our favorite place. Jessica spread the blanket on the sand and we sat and waited for the sun to rise.

"What are we going to do if I am pregnant? We can't have a baby all by ourselves."

As if to contradict that observation, we made love on the beach before paddling home.

"We're going into town early. You can visit the doctor while I find the library and read up on home birthing. Maybe the librarian will know a nurse," I said.

"I think the doctor should know all the nurses. The town isn't that big, Russell."

"When do you want to go?"

"Can we wait a few days?" she asked. I'm still in shock. I want to be sure I miss my next one, too."

"But that's two weeks away." I almost shouted.

"Yes, it is. I want to be sure. And so do you, even if you won't admit it."

We spent an idyllic two weeks, lost in our very own paradise. I think we were both taken by surprise at the pregnancy. After all, we'd never talked beyond surviving the troubles. We readily adopted and adapted to a foreign country. We never once discussed returning home.

As far as I was concerned, there was nothing to return to.

Now, with the coming addition to our family of two, we looked at our present situation from an entirely new perspective. In another seven or eight months, if it hadn't already happened with Jessica's announcement, our lives would change again, forever, and in a most dramatic way.

We spent the next weeks discussing and comparing family medical histories just like a regular couple planning on having a baby. All this hadn't been covered by any of the reading I did to prepare for the trip across the border, and probably just as well.

It would have scared me to death.

21

Paradise Lost

Our next trip into town wasn't coming soon enough as far as I was concerned. While I tried to while away the days, I came up with what I knew was a fantastic plan for Jessica once we made it to Loreto. Implementation would be easy.

I'd leave her at the market while sneaking away using one feeble excuse or another, maybe baked bread, or gas if we took the truck into town. I'd pick up a couple of items including the bread and slip them into my bag. I'd pick up flowers, too. I could stow it all in the front of our kayak.

As it turned out, all my planning went for naught. We went into town early. I managed to get away and pick up everything. It ended up being a long paddle home waiting to spring my surprise.

Just before dinner I pulled out the flowers. Jessica blushed and smiled and fussed with her hair and I pretty much had it made. We shared our dinner of fish and potatoes baked in the fire and the fresh vegetables we picked up in town. The sun was setting behind us over the hills and it was starting to get dark beneath our little overhang.

I presented Jessica with the gift-wrapped present. Her enthusiasm to undo the wrapping only encouraged me. I just knew she'd like what was inside. She tore at the paper and studied the print on the boxes. She looked at me, horrified.

Right off I knew I made a huge mistake.

"I've already made an appointment at the hospital in town. They're going to poke and probe and examine and test and do whatever has to be done to tell me what I already know."

"But I thought you'd like to know before you went in."

"I'm not like that, Russell. I want to be just as surprised as you were at my announcement. If I go in already knowing, what's to do? The outcome would have been foretold."

"Well—" I was flummoxed.

"I know. You thought you were doing the right thing. Well, you were. It's just not the right thing for me."

"I'm sorry. I thought—"

"In case you're left wondering, you're going to be right there with me to hold my hand—and anything else of mine that needs holding."

"I am?"

"You are. Thank you for the flowers. They're beautiful."

Jessica got up. By the time she finished, her naked silhouette enticed me into carrying her into the tent.

"At the end of this, there won't be much love-making going on—or much of anything else, either. I'm probably going to be too stressed about hurting the baby."

"You think I won't be? I'll be a nervous wreck."

We kissed and made up with enthusiastic, desperate lovemaking and fell asleep in each other's arms.

The day began with plenty of blue sky and sunshine. According to Jessica's forecast, it would soon be replaced with low cloud and a cold wind. I had no reason to doubt her so I suggested we take the truck into town.

Instead, we kayaked, and the effort fighting with wind ensured we'd take time to grab something at a taquería. I walked with Jessica to the hospital and made sure she was settled with the paperwork in the small waiting room.

She didn't appear upset when I told her I had to pick up another surprise. She gave me the look and then smiled and waved me off.

I exited through the hospital parking lot. A familiar-looking truck caught my eye. It couldn't be. Immediately I put it out of my mind. I just didn't want to deal with it right now. Already I had more to worry about than I wanted. My concern for Jessica's health and how we'd manage to fit a baby into our lives on a Baja beach was paramount.

I located the shop in the town's small downtown and hurried back to the hospital. Jessica wasn't in the waiting room. She had to be undergoing her examination.

"I thought that was you out in the parking lot. What are you doing here?"

The voice was familiar. Caitrin. Shocked, I turned toward it. "I have the same question. What are you doing here?" I couldn't believe it. The woman disappeared, and now here she was at the very place where I didn't want to see her ever again.

"I come in three days a week. I wanted to give something back for being allowed into the country," she explained.

I didn't volunteer I'd hooked up with Jessica. In fact, I'd be damned if I'd volunteer anything to Caitrin. I hurried past her into Jessica's room. I presented her with the packages of flower seeds.

"Are these supposed to make up for Caitrin being here?"

"You saw her."

Jessica didn't look happy. "Yes, I saw her. She made a point of saying hello like we were besties. Now what?"

I could tell Jessica was more than a little annoyed.

"We're not leaving until I have my ultra-sound. Not a word to her about my pregnancy. None. Understand? I don't trust her. I wouldn't put it past her to be stalking us."

"Seriously? I never thought that about her."

"You've known her longer than I have, yes, but I don't think you ever saw her dark side until she got down on her knees for Todd."

That was true, I had to admit. But doubts about Caitrin's fickle nature after that happened were only reinforced. "You're probably right. In fact, I almost know it. She never did tell me much about her life prior to meeting me. Now that I think about it, she hooked me like a fish."

"I know you don't want to hear it, Russell, but we're going to have to keep an eye out for that woman. If she is stalking us, it could mean we're going to have to move."

"I'm not moving. Neither are you. Unless you plan on hitchhiking away from me. Are you?"

"Of course not. I love you. And we're having our

baby. But if that woman attempts to insert herself into the good life we've found together, she doesn't know what she's in for."

Jessica's concern was clear. Even the tone of her voice had hardened. Were I Caitrin, I wouldn't be messing with Jessica. With us.

"I wonder if Todd is still around. Her truck is pretty beat up. Maybe he wrecked it and she ditched him."

"Why don't you do some kissing up and try to find out? I have to wait for my prescription."

I looked at her askance. "Did I just hear you right? You want me to see her?" This couldn't be good. Jessica's answer was one word.

"Yes."

Okay. So maybe it wouldn't be all bad, then.

I had no memory of mentioning anything to Jessica about the gold Caitrin supposedly found back in the city. She made a big deal of allowing me to see it when we were in our house. If she told Todd about it in an attempt to convince him to hook up with her, I wouldn't put it past him to try to steal it.

Gold and a blow job can be pretty convincing, especially when they come with the same woman. I know it was that way for me. I was certain Todd would have considered it a golden blow job, if nothing else. I snickered at my joke.

I tracked Caitrin to the hallway where Jessica's examining room was located. She was walking out of it.

"She's pregnant. Why didn't you tell me, Russell?"

Shit. Now she was making it sound like she wanted to be kept up to date about what was happening with the guy she'd screwed over.

"Because it's none of your business, that's why. What happened to Todd? Is he here with you?"

"He stole all my money and deserted me. The only reason I have the truck is because I hid the keys away and wouldn't tell him where they were. He turned out to be a jerk."

"Just as you thought about me when you were waving goodbye. Funny how that works, isn't it? It's old news, according to Jessica. She was capable of reading him right. She was pretty happy when you took him off her hands."

"She must have been. Look who she ended up with. You're a good provider, Russell. I tried to do right by you, you know."

"Except for that missing bra and Todd's come stains all over the front of your shirt. You couldn't swallow fast enough for him, or what?"

She turned beet red.

I wouldn't let it go. "Maybe if you got to know him a little better before you ran off, things between us might have turned out differently." I regretted the words as soon as they came out. I wasn't concerned for Caitrin any longer. She eroded any trust when she ran off with a stranger. My concerns were for Jessica and our child.

"I've got to go. Jessica is waiting."

I checked the reflections in the sliding doors of the hospital on our way out. Just as I thought, Caitrin had positioned herself to keep an eye on us.

"That woman is going to be trouble. I know it."

"She's not going to hurt us, Russell. I can guarantee that."

We paddled back to camp. The whole time we worked out a strategy that would keep us aware of our surroundings and anyone that intruded. Our idyllic life would continue.

Jessica and I were happy. We were getting to know one another even better. We were content with our surroundings. We were intent on not letting anyone come between us or the life we worked so hard for.

Jessica planted the Geranium seeds. Beautiful long-lasting flowers in a brilliant variety of colors lent an air of house and home to our palapa. The campsite was a picture of happiness. We laughed and were content with our good fortune. We waited on pins and needles for anything from Caitrin.

Weeks passed. Our routines by now became well established. We fished. We explored on foot. We went on picnics. We made sure our site would give us plenty of warning if anyone tried to come up on us at night.

Caitrin had to be behind me. Behind us. I was certain. Jessica wasn't. Even so, I became engrossed in my own happy life with Jessica. I wouldn't let her discuss what would happen if Caitrin showed up.

I wasn't ready for any interruption to our idyllic life.

It happened sooner than either of us thought. In fact, I was still unconvinced Caitrin would be interested in us in the slightest. Why would she? She had been the one to desert me. She made her choice and was living by it.

"She's here." Jessica was convinced.

I wasn't.

"What? No way." I didn't want to believe it.

"Don't look around. I'm telling you she's up on the hill by the road. I saw a reflection. I think she's watching us with binoculars."

"I'm going to talk to her."

"No. You're not. You're not going to do anything. We're going to go on like nothing is happening."

"Jessica—" I began.

"No. Trust me. I said I'd handle it and I will."

"You say that now, but if you were eight or nine months pregnant, what would you be able to do? And you will be nine months pregnant much too soon. What if she shows up then?"

"I caught that woman looking at the ultrasound printouts," she told me. "She's jealous."

I shook my head. "Jealous? Of what? She has nothing to be jealous about."

Jessica gave me a look that would have turned me into a block of ice if she could. "She sees you as having everything. When she screwed off with Todd, she ended up with a broken-down truck and a huge pile of nothing. He screwed off just when she thought he'd be taking her to a better place. Surely even you must see how that didn't work out for the woman."

Jessica was right. Caitrin was probably in desperate straits now that she didn't have a partner.

"Then it's even more dangerous for you. She sees you as having stolen everything from her. From what you're saying, now she wants it back. All of it."

I looked at Jessica with a new understanding.

"Now you're getting it. I don't think we'll have long to wait before it comes to a head."

"What the hell is that supposed to mean?" I asked her.

She stared at me for too long. "It means she'll be coming at me like a freight train."

We drove into town rather than fight the wind and the waves in the kayak. I parked in the hospital lot and walked in with Jessica to wait in the small waiting room.

"I'm going to do some shopping so we don't get home late and have to wipe out our tracks in the dark," I told her. We still swept out any sign with palm leaves every time we drove down the hill. We could only hope no one noticed the tracks until we returned and repeated the deed.

"I might take a walk for the exercise. If not, I'll be in the waiting room."

I stopped at the glass door. Someone had opened a door on our truck and was searching it. I held off running out. If it was a case of some chapulino with a gun looking to steal a truck, I didn't want to get shot. If it was policía, they'd no doubt find me when they were ready.

In that case, I was prepared for a long wait, until the intruder straightened. It was Caitrin. So Jessica was right all along.

I headed out to the truck to confront the woman. "What are you doing?"

She straightened. She looked guilty of something. Come to think of it, she looked guilty every time I saw her in Loreto. Why did I never notice that before?

"Oh. Hi. I was looking for something I left in your truck. I can't find my passport and I thought it might still be there."

I knew that to be a lie. For sure it wasn't in the glove box, because I cleaned that out ages ago. I tossed everything that might have belonged to her. The passport wasn't there.

"So you're heading farther south into Central

America?" I asked. I really did want to know. Jessica would be relieved once I told her.

"I'm getting tired of hanging around here. I need a change."

And a new sucker, too, probably. With some money, if I knew her. "I'll help you look."

I went through the truck, keeping an eye on Caitrin. I didn't trust her any more since Jessica convinced me she could be a danger to both of us. I was never a believer in woman's intuition, but with Jessica and now our baby to worry about, it was a good time to start.

"It's not here, Caitrin." Thank goodness. Jessica would be pissed if she knew I helped this woman find her passport in what was now our truck.

"Okay. Well, thanks for the help."

She walked over to her beat up truck and headed for the parking lot exit. Caitrin smiled and waved before pulling out onto the street. I didn't believe for one minute that the smile was genuine.

Now I had to decide whether to tell Jessica about finding Caitrin going through our truck. It wouldn't sit well with her.

Our idyllic life continued uninterrupted by Caitrin. We decided we couldn't and wouldn't let her insert herself into our lives, no matter what. That she seemed to have forgotten about us didn't hurt, either. I started to think I was right after all.

On our next hospital visit, I made sure to sweet-talk one of the nurses. In my broken Spanish I convinced the woman, through much nodding and smiling, that I needed to know Caitrin's schedule. She happily handed over the shift sheet, and I smiled and nodded my gracias.

From then on, we made certain our trips to the small hospital for doctor's visits were completed around the days Caitrin was away.

Jessica's pregnancy continued trouble-free. When she didn't want to go into town for a checkup because she was feeling fine, I got on her case until she agreed.

Whatever strange or unusual food she developed a craving for, I managed to find. I drew the line at pickled fish with onions and sour cream, but only because I couldn't find any pickled fish. I was forced to admit I hit my limit. She never asked again, and I stopped looking.

When Caitrin's shift changed, the nurse I made the original deal with waved me over and passed the time sheet. We made arrangements to get around her.

Jessica was happy. I was happy. The life growing in her seemed to be content and happy too, growing faster than we both wanted. So it was, one late night, when I wasn't prepared for Jessica's urgent shaking. I mumbled and tossed and woke up to a hand covering my mouth.

"Listen. Can you hear it?"

"No. What? Give me a chance to wake up, at least." I mumbled past her hand and she took it away from my mouth.

"Someone must have kicked one of our strings. The cans rattled down the rock face."

No way. Could Caitrin be that stupid or delusional?

"Jessica. It's the wind. Listen." The palms rustled above us. Waves slapped at the shore. I couldn't hear a thing beyond that. "You're imagining it. What are you doing?"

Jessica was already out of bed and throwing on black pants and a shirt. She groaned while bending over to do up her boot laces. "Are you coming with me or not?"

"Dammit woman, you will stay right here and not move a muscle until I get back. Or else." I exited the tent and crawled beneath the truck. I retrieved my sawed-off and the bandolier of shells.

"I didn't know you had that."

"For emergencies only. I know you're not going to stay here by yourself. Here's what we're going to do."

22

Trouble

I hugged the base of the hill. I wanted to remain unseen at least until the last possible moment. I needed to make my way undiscovered up the steep, rough road to the highway turnout. From there, I would be able to descend undetected until I got close to Caitrin. If it was Caitrin.

I still had my doubts.

Perhaps I should have known better, but I pretty much convinced myself that Caitrin was harmless. After all we went through as a team, I didn't think she had any intent to hurt either of us. Why would she? She left me before I knew Jessica. I even remember her telling me Jessica was a nobody.

I stumbled on a rock and fell to my knees. If I didn't stop thinking about the woman, I'd give myself away. I concentrated on climbing the hill in the dark.

It was no picnic. By the time I huffed and puffed my way to the top and discovered the woman's truck, I knew I was wrong. She had a huge head-start down the cliff face.

Should I stay and chase after Caitrin, not knowing whether Jessica would be able to handle her? Or should I get rid of the truck first and any evidence she had ever been here?

If I thought about it, getting rid of the truck would mean I'd have to take Caitrin out of the picture. I don't think I fully realized what that would entail. Surely it wasn't at the point of being so bad between us that I had to consider doing the woman harm.

If the woman made it down the hill and ended up confronting Jessica, I had no idea what the outcome would be. I wasn't sure Jessica would prevail. Would there be a fight to the death, or would there only be a confrontation and a whole lot of yelling and screaming?

Then I remembered the k-bar Caitrin always carried when we were in the city. It might not be a good idea to underestimate her after all.

Was Jessica up to the task, either way? I didn't know. I only knew I wanted safety for her and for our unborn baby. That meant I had to get to Caitrin sooner rather than later.

The cloud cover broke and opened up, revealing the moon. I caught a quick glimpse of Caitrin half-way down the hill. She was taking her time, treading carefully around large boulders. She zig-zagged as best she could, helped by the sudden appearance of the moon.

I knew what I had to do.

Slowly and with great care, I closed the distance between us. It wasn't easy. The hill was steep in places. Loose rock was everywhere. Sometimes I had to climb up to go down.

As I grew closer, I heard Caitrin's labored breathing

and grunts as she climbed over boulders. She was that determined to get to our campsite. She had to be thinking we'd both be there, blissfully unaware that she was bearing down on us.

She made her way over the raised patches of bare rock that made for difficult going. I avoided doing the same. I didn't want her to know I was gaining. If she learned I was above her, would that change her mind?

Jessica remained out of sight. I hoped she would stay where she was supposed to. If I knew her, she had Caitrin in sight and was watching her make her way downslope to the rocky beach beneath the hill. The rocks and stones crunching underfoot would announce her arrival at sea level. If Jessica wasn't paying attention and the woman managed to make it to the sand, she'd have no warning.

I silently prayed Jessica was paying attention.

The moon ducked behind an errant cloud and then reappeared. Caitrin halted and turned to look up the hill. I froze, not taking my eyes off her. There was no mistaking it. She was hell-bent on sneaking up on our campsite.

The woman definitely meant business. In profile I could make out the shotgun strung across her back. It wasn't as clear, but it looked like the bandolier hung down in front.

As far as I was concerned, none of it was good.

Jessica proved to be right again.

I ran through everything I should have told Jessica. The list was short. It consisted of one item—where to find the firearms I stashed away beneath the truck's box. Now that I knew Caitrin carried her shotgun, I had to get to her before she found Jessica.

"I can see you, bitch."

I recognized Jessica's voice. She must have spotted Caitrin outlined against the thin cloud obscuring the moon. She wouldn't know that Caitrin brought her shotgun along.

"That's all right. You're going to see hell a lot sooner," Caitrin called to her.

The action on the double-barreled shotgun clicked, and I knew it was closed. Surely Jessica heard it, too. The crunching rocks at the base of the cliff announced she had moved closer for shelter. Every step she took would be broadcast to Caitrin.

"Jessica!" I screamed. Get to the truck. There's a shotgun under the box in front of the fuel tank. "You'll need a light to see it."

I listened to her gallop across the rock base. Caitrin halted, straightened, and pulled the trigger on her shotgun. The boom echoed off the face of the cliff and out over the water. There was no denying it now. The woman meant business. I had to get to her before she got to Jessica.

Silence followed. A light illuminated the sand beneath the truck. Jessica made it. I heard cursing and my name and then nothing. "Got it! Ouch! What—"

Finally. The light stayed beneath the truck for longer than I wanted. "It's loaded."

"Stay by the truck," I called to her. "Caitrin has a shotgun."

"In that case, we're gonna have a Mexican standoff going on." Then, louder. "Bring it on, you fucking bitch."

One thing about Jessica. She was no shrinking violet.

She fired a round into the face of the cliff. Then another. In the dead night air Jessica's double barrel breeched, and then firmly closed a moment later. She was reloaded.

"Caitrin. Give it up. Jessica is armed. You'll never do it."

I had no idea what the woman intended for us. I went with kill. Maim or wound was far down the list. Any hope I had she might be attempting to frighten us went out the window and splashed into the Golfo.

How could I be so wrong about the woman I trusted with my life only months earlier?

The commotion and the gunfire must have distracted Caitrin. Maybe it forced her to think. She remained where she was, hesitating, perhaps thinking about changing her mind. By then I caught up to her. Five more feet and I'd be directly behind her.

I don't know if I did it on purpose. All I knew for sure was that I didn't want anything to happen to Jessica and our baby. I reached out with both hands. I took a step back for leverage. A rock bounced away and down the cliff.

Caitrin chose that instant to turn. Surprised and finally realizing that I wasn't with Jessica, she screamed. "You bastard. Where's the rest of my gold?"

I stumbled and brushed against her. My hip caught hers as she toppled to the ground. I went down hard beside her. The double-barrel 12-gauge boomed in a single explosion, deafening me.

Caitrin fought to get up. Unsteady on both feet in the darkness, she fumbled with her bandolier. She searched for cartridges. The shotgun clicked. She was reloaded.

I kicked at what I hoped was a knee. It barely connected. It was just enough to unbalance her.

She went sideways.

The shotgun boomed again with both barrels.

The recoil knocked her backwards.

Caitrin screamed.

Her feet kicked.

Her arms flailed.

The shotgun fell to the ground and clattered down the face of the cliff.

It all happened in slow motion.

Unable to maintain her balance on the sloping ground, she screamed again.

She reached out in an attempt to grab onto me.

I reached for her.

It was futile.

Grasping fingers brushed mine and then slipped away.

A heel caught on a boulder.

That was all it took. Caitrin flew backwards off the cliff.

Her screams echoed. Her arms flailed all the way down. A solid thump confirmed she landed on the boulder-strewn rubble at the base of the cliff. I stood up and yelled to Jessica. "She's down. Go check on her. Be careful."

Why that last, I didn't know. There was no way anyone could survive a fall from that height. Jessica didn't answer me. "Are you there? Are you all right? Jess?"

I continued snaking my way down the face of the cliff. I stumbled and fell onto my already bruised knees. I cursed. I stumbled again. I cursed louder.

"Jess?" Why didn't she answer? I screamed again. "Jess!"

I couldn't contain my growing sense of panic. What the hell? Had Caitrin landed on her? Where the hell was she?

"I'm all right, Russell."

Finally.

"She won't bother us any more."

Exhausted, I went to my knees. "And it's Jessica. How soon you forget."

"Woman, you know how to put fear into a man's heart."

23

Falling

I made my way carefully down the rough, rocky cliff face in inky blackness. I made it to the base in time to make out Jessica still bent over Caitrin. She looked up at me and shook her head. "Nothing. She's gone."

I didn't want to believe it. "Are you sure?"

Desperation in my voice warned Jessica. She checked again. "Yes. There's no pulse." She checked a third time.

Physically exhausted, I exhaled and collapsed to sit on a rock. "Shit. Now we have a body. The policía aren't going to take kindly to a trio of gringos when one of them is dead."

Jessica sat down beside me on the rock. We were breathing heavily. The shock of what happened completely overtook our senses. I wanted to at least appear positive in an impossible situation. "She wasn't successful, whatever she was trying to do to us. We're both alive and unhurt." Maybe it was too soon to be so optimistic. I didn't think so.

"You're right," Jessica reassured me.

I was about to hug Jessica when she uttered the sentence I was incapable of saying.

"We have a body to dispose of."

We were about to jeopardize everything we worked so hard for. Even in death Caitrin continued to threaten us.

I helped the woman I loved up off the rock.

"Come on, we need to do something right away."

Jessica leaned heavily against me. Even though the huge weight bearing down on us was lifted, we now had to struggle through one more trial. Our lives were no longer happy or simple.

With Jessica still in shock, we struggled to our campsite carting the lifeless, heavy body. We made it to the palapa where we collapsed in each other's arms.

But for Jessica's vigilance, we would probably be preparing to move out.

Neither of us uttered a word. We collapsed in the tent.

Jessica shivered and shook and I tried to quietly comfort her. I almost succeeded until I began doing the same.

Eventually, completely exhausted emotionally and physically, we fell into fitful sleep in each other's arms.

I left Jessica sleeping. I got up and wrestled and rolled Caitrin's body into a blue plastic tarp. With shaking hands, I wrapped rope around the formless body of a woman I once cared for very deeply. The task completed, I cleaned up and prepared for our day.

It was going to be a long one.

Still on edge and uneasy, I cleaned up and bent to the task of preparing sandwiches for what I knew would be a backbreaking exercise that couldn't be avoided. I added plenty of bottled water and packed it all away in the kayak's front storage.

Jessica was sleeping soundly. I was reluctant to wake her. Were it not for what had to be done, I would have left her that way. I shook her gently and her eyes opened immediately. She smiled up at me, looking frail.

"It's time. We have no other choice. We have to get out on the water right away. The kayak is ready. I made us sandwiches for later. It's going to be a very long day." Almost as an afterthought, I added a final statement as a matter of fact. "Caitrin's body is already rigged. We're going to tow her out."

There was no doubt we were in this to the end. Jessica said nothing. She appeared to be in shock. She looked at me, pale and subdued, and began going through the motions of dressing herself like a robot. I helped tie her boots and fastened her life jacket.

"We have to do it. If we're going to stay here, we have no choice." I didn't know what else to say.

"You're right. It was no fault of ours. What about her truck?"

"While you were sleeping, I moved it miles down the road. I punched a hole in the gas tank and set fire to it. It should be a burned-out shell by now. I didn't tell her I had to go through Caitrin's pockets for the keys.

"What about her shotgun?"

It was already on board the kayak. I had wiped the shotgun down, just in case. It was one of my more lucid thoughts since destroying the truck.

"We'll dump that, too. When we get back, I'll do a walk-through of the route she took down the face of the cliff to look for anything else. That has to be done in daylight.

We'd have more time then. Now all I wanted was get rid of the most inconvenient evidence that anyone had ever been here. Jessica trembled and shook her head. She wouldn't look at me.

"What else can we do, Jessica? She would have used that shotgun on us. We protected ourselves from harm. If we go to the police, we'll be the ones sitting in jail. We need this country right now, even if it doesn't need us. We might need it forever."

"You're right. And I agree. It's just—"

"I know, sweetheart. I know. This isn't any easier for me."

Yet it was. In my heart of hearts, I knew if we didn't handle it, we'd be in more trouble than we could imagine. We were in a foreign country. We had no idea of the justice system, other than what we heard by way of rumor and what we witnessed.

The language difference had us at a complete disadvantage. We were basically broke. We wouldn't be capable of bribing anyone. If there was something I left out, I couldn't know.

I wrestled the body into the water until it floated. I secured the tow rope to the kayak, and at high tide I pushed us off and we began paddling to save our lives. The blue tarp ended up floating inches below the surface.

Jessica looked back over her shoulder at our campsite. It was as though she was taking one last look before beginning another journey. And I suppose we were on another journey, only this time, we'd be back to where we started. I only hoped she wouldn't want to move on again.

Perhaps I was being naïve. I felt we could make a go of it right where we were. It had everything. Nothing changed that. And then Caitrin came along to screw it all up, just as she had back in L.A. when she tripped and stumbled into my life.

I had willingly let her then, of course. This time, she somehow convinced herself she needed to be a part of our lives. It was crazy. She was crazy. And now my carefree existence with Jessica was threatened and would no doubt end up paying the price.

I knew I'd have a fight on my hands to convince Jessica to stay. We'd fought so hard, together, finally overcoming Caitrin's intrusion into our lives. Would we be able to accept what happened and eventually move on?

The Golfo sun beat down relentlessly. There was barely a wind to help us. At least with no waves to fight against, the kayak cut through the water easily.

"How much farther?" Jessica asked. "I'm exhausted."

I turned to look. We were still within sight of our campground. I sighed and resumed paddling. "We need to keep going. We have to get out into the current. That's why I brought food and water."

Already I suspected we'd be on the Golfo all day. Quite possibly we wouldn't get back to the palapa until well after dark. I didn't let on. I wanted Jessica to concentrate on the job. It had to get done.

By late afternoon I had enough, too. I was tired and moody and exhausted and covered in sweat under the hot sun. The Golfo was beginning to kick up wind and salt spray. Too exhausted to even speak, I tapped Jessica on the shoulder with the paddle and she allowed herself to collapse over the front rigging.

"Hang onto the paddle. It'll take us twice as long to

get home if it drifts away."

I let her take a break while I tugged the tarp with Caitrin's body closer to the kayak. I sliced the nylon rope and watched the weak gulf current slowly float her away.

Good riddance.

When I was satisfied, I gave the shotgun a final wipe-down and tossed it overboard. It plopped into the water and sank out of sight.

It was done. Would Jessica be done with me? I hoped not. I tried to relax as I rigged the small mid-kayak sail for home. I left Jessica resting over the bow. She didn't move for the longest time and I wondered what she was thinking.

We must have sailed for a good hour or more before she finally sat up and came back to me. Talk about the simple things, but it made me happy when she opened the bow hatch and dug inside for the cheese and sandwiches I stowed away. She smiled faintly when she recognized the sail and realized she no longer had to paddle.

We celebrated with water and more sunscreen.

That our idyllic lifestyle had been sadly interrupted and finally reduced to nothing by the crazy Caitrin hadn't been lost on me. I knew now there was no way in hell that either of us would want to remain camped on our present ground.

We'd need a new location, one that was far away from our present circumstance. We needed time to forget and to heal, happy memories of our present location be damned.

It was past dark when the kayak scraped shore beneath the high cloud hiding the moon. I recognized our location as being a couple of miles from our palapa. I was happy that we were close to home. We walked the distance while towing the kayak in the shallow water.

In the dim light of dawn, the flowers Jessica planted waved a welcome in the breeze coming in off the gulf. We collapsed in our tent, disrobed, and fell into mad, sweaty, frenzied lovemaking. We used one another in an attempt to force the events of the previous day and night out of our thoughts.

Dead End

I lay awake and tried not to think of a future clouded by what happened in our own country. I had to start thinking about what Jessica and I had to do to ensure our continued safety in the foreign country we adopted.

If only we weren't discovered, if we kept our hands clean and stayed off the grid, we'd be home free. But how long would that last if Caitrin's body floated ashore? It would be plainly evident to the policía that whoever bundled up a woman in a blue tarp and towed her offshore to drift in the current obviously had something to hide.

Surely the investigators would show around a picture of the corpse. If she was recognizable, someone somewhere would remember the good-looking woman that had last been seen making her way down the Baja in a convoy of two well-equipped trucks.

The burned-out shell by the side of the highway would perhaps be recognized for what it was. How long would it be before detectives made their way down to our campsite and begin to ask questions?

A new plan forced its way into my thoughts. Maybe not the best. Perhaps not the most enlightened. But it sure beat trying to listen to the radio to find out if any random floaters had shown up in the Golfo.

Would Jessica support me in its implementation?

It would mean packing up a final time and heading north. True, we'd be backtracking. Also true, we'd be leaving behind the safety and comfort of the forever-scarred campsite we had grown to love.

What else could we do? If conditions changed for the better north of the border, if we could find out what was going on, if we'd be safe, we'd be home-free.

It was a lot of ifs. It would mean deserting our own perfect world in our new country. While Caitrin's death had certainly scarred it, we hadn't done anything anyone else wouldn't have done to protect their own family.

Would the trip home be worth the effort?

There was nothing on the radio bands from up north. No AM/FM, digital or any other signals. Anyone we talked to said the same thing. There was no outward sign of any change.

Still, I thought we should make an attempt. We needed to find out. Otherwise, I was certain it would eat away at us, finally destroying everything we were working so hard toward.

We argued back and forth, although it wasn't really an argument. It was more of a series of discussions that turned into arguments. While at first she didn't want to even talk about it, slowly Jessica warmed to the idea when I brought the baby we were going to have into the conversation.

Perhaps it was unfair, but that's what won her over. I

asked if it could be possible to have our baby born on home soil. I explained it wasn't like I was expecting a birth certificate and an entry in a passport. It was simpler than that. It was the idea, the possibility.

Which, when I put it to Jessica that way, she went for it.

"Then I think we should. It will give us a reason to get away from here. If we have to come back, we'll have plenty of time to reconsider on the way."

If we come back.

"Do you think it possible that anything has changed back home?" Home. It had been. Was it still?

"How will we know unless we try?"

"In that case, we'll retrace our steps to Tecate," she agreed.

How bad could it be?

Jessica brightened at the idea, and then indicated I should follow her to the little waterfall trickling out of the rock face. Fresh water was the one thing that helped us decide on staying here and making a home.

"There's something I've been meaning to tell you."

She hesitated just long enough for my heart to skip a beat before she went on. "When I was beneath the truck trying to find the shotgun—"

"You banged your head and started cursing like a drunken sailor. I remember my name being bandied about." I never heard her swear before. At the time, I took it in stride, all things considered with the stress of Caitrin's attack in the dark of night.

"Well, there's one more thing. I didn't exactly bang my head. Something fell out of your box and smacked me a good one."

Jessica halted at a small indentation in the rock face. A

cloud of sand flew as she scratched and dug it away with her hands. The grin glued to her face was so intense I thought she must have discovered a pirate's buried treasure.

It was better than that. Jessica slammed at least twenty gold bars on our small table. It had to be at least half of what Caitrin brought with us on our trip south. No wonder the woman wanted to reconnect.

Jessica and I usually kayaked to and from the clinic. The one time we arrived in the truck, Caitrin was out searching it for booty. That's when I came along and caught her. She had to figure out a way to get to the gold and get rid of any witnesses.

That was why she was coming down the face of the cliff. The element of surprise would make sure she caught us off guard. After doing whatever it was she wanted to do to us, she'd be able to thoroughly search our truck.

Maybe it was luck that brought her to the cliff after all. Now we didn't need to worry over a single thing. We had enough money to live on the Baja forever.

Even with all that, our plan to head home didn't take a back seat.

The weather stayed sunny and mild. We began packing up, a bit at a time, as though reluctant to follow through. When we figured out it was going to take us forever, the reluctance turned into a frenzy to get done and get on the road.

Most goods ended up stowed on the truck. Of course, there would never be enough room without the trailer we decided to leave behind. If we got home, I was certain that there would be plenty of places for us to move into, for surely the crisis continued in some way.

Several of Jessica's gold bars ended up back where she stashed them by the spring water. It would be there if disaster in some form struck and we needed to return. I never told her about it. Whether it meant that I didn't believe we'd get home, I didn't know.

The half-ton labored up the steep trail it had so easily descended with the trailer in tow when we first found the spot. Perhaps it was reluctant to leave, too. I caught Jessica looking out over the Golfo and back at our hidden campsite.

"We can still change our minds," I told her.

"Yes. We can. But we need to know what's happening with our country."

There was little traffic headed north. Almost none, in fact. We didn't stop to talk to anyone. We didn't want to become disillusioned. We didn't want to question the wisdom of our decision. Learning that nothing had changed would only make us miserable. We were miserable enough following our kayaking expedition to float Caitrin's body away.

By the end of the day our expectations were enormous. We talked about our excitement. About how great it was going to be home, in our own country. About our plans to live together and raise our child.

On the edge of Tecate, I slowed and pulled into a Pemex. I fueled and then slowly drove toward the border. The cambio had been repaired. There was no sign of the explosion when we first crossed the border. Freshly painted green and white walls gleamed as we drove slowly past.

Then our gaze moved toward the border in front of us.

"What the? Jessica. Look."

I parked and got out. I crossed over to open Jessica's door and helped her and her growing baby bump out of the truck. I managed to catch her before she slipped to her knees.

"Come on, girl. We have to be strong for each other."

She looked at me. A shocked expression turned into one of questioning. It remained on her face as she looked from me to the border and back. "What does it mean?"

We studied the border we had so easily and hastily crossed only months before. I could only imagine what it meant.

The road to the border on the Mexican side dead-ended suddenly. Huge cement and steel barriers blocked access. Nothing on wheels could proceed. Foot traffic would be halted by rows of razor wire. A wide swath across the marker had been cleared of vegetation and graded flat by huge earth movers, judging by the many deep tracks.

The empty space of no-man's-land the earth movers left behind looked to be about a quarter-mile deep. Hills had been graded flat. Long, deep rows of barbed wire alternating with razor wire ran in parallel lines that disappeared into infinity both east and west.

Multiple rotating cameras mounted on light standards stood sentry. What appeared to be razor-sharp spikes poked out from the top of the gray wall. More razor wire hung off the wall and topped the spikes.

We took it in, not quite sure what we were seeing. A lot of work had been done since we crossed, that was certain. Who did it? How had it been accomplished so fast? Was the border with Canada and Alaska done in the same fashion? Did the wall run the entire length of the border with Mexico? These were questions for which we had no answers.

More than likely, never would.

Our initial shock slowly subsided. We found renewed strength in each other. Arm in arm, we returned to the truck. We took one last look at the fortress surrounded by razor wire and gray concrete, knowing full well we would never see it again.

"We're not wanted. We need to get back on the road before the Mexicans change their mind the way America has."

"Russell—"

"We'll be all right. We're a family now. We have to be strong for all three of us when you-know-who arrives."

Jessica slid over in the seat and settled against me. Her head rested on my shoulder.

"Don't forget your seatbelt. We're going to live a long time and raise a hockey team."

Jessica looked at me, dubious, to say the least. "Hockey? Where are we going to get skates in Mexico, dear? We'll have a baseball team." She kissed my cheek.

"A baseball team?"

"Yes. It'll take a while, but I think we're both up to it."

And so it was decided. So much for an idyllic lifestyle as a beach bum. I had been committed to being a baseball coach by the love of my life. "Whatever you say, dear."

In the mirror Jessica rolled her eyes. She grinned and kissed me again.

"I'm thinking that by number four or five, if not sooner, you'll be too exhausted for anything more than sleeping with your back to me," I said.

A mischievous look crossed her face and remained there. "Well, we can try doing it that way. If it doesn't work, we can experiment to find out what we both like. If not, we can go back to the boring missionary position. Eventually."

25

Nadja

Our most recent trip took us north to the border. We hoped to reconcile with a country in extreme distress. We wanted to ensure our baby would be born at home, our home, in our country. The wall we encountered was no welcome mat, and indeed, it was greeted with dismay.

It was a huge, Not welcome keep out, sign.

We didn't bother to knock. In any case, there was nowhere to knock. The multiple seamless barriers of razor wire and concrete and steel made sure of that. It was meant to keep anyone and everyone out, including citizens.

It was most likely keeping anyone left behind in, as well, but that was more than I wanted to think about. On seeing the impediment, neither Jessica nor I cared any more. We realized just how fortunate we were to have escaped, and in the nick of time.

That foreboding gray wall convinced us to never return.

Suitably chastened at the sight of the monstrosity confronting us, we began our return to our residence on the Golfo, half-way down the peninsula. Not for one instant did we consider we were doomed. We stopped in Ensenada to do some shopping and spend the night.

In Santo Tomás, we celebrated our good fortune at having met one another by having a late lunch in the small restaurant where I first convinced Jessica that we should travel together.

"I knew you were going to be trouble. That's why I kept my distance."

"You didn't keep much distance once you tore down the blanket dividing the tent," I reminded her. I reached to rub Jessica's very pregnant stomach. She sighed and we smiled happily.

"Well, it was cold and I was covered in goosebumps. I needed warming up."

"No you didn't. And those goosebumps weren't from being cold, either."

Jessica blushed. "Well, you were a good bed-warmer. What can I say?"

"You can start by not denying you only wanted me for a taxi-ride to the next town big enough for you to survive in," I said.

"Which must have been the reason why I ended up naked and willing on an isolated sand beach waiting for you to get your rear end and everything else down to me."

"If I didn't love you—" I began.

"If we didn't love each other—"

"We'd be in big trouble," I finished for both of us.

We were happy on the Bahía. We had food fresh from the Golfo. A huge palapa over our home shaded us from the elements. We kept up with preparations for the baby that would soon be arriving.

Jessica continued with her appointments in the capable, small-town hospital to the north. The plan was to paddle back and forth in the kayak until the very end. She'd have the baby in our home, or, given enough warning, I'd drive her to the hospital to give birth.

I didn't want to let on, but I very much wanted a hospital birth. I knew how disappointed Jessica would be if she knew that. In the long run it would be safer knowing that doctors and nurses would be present in the event of problems.

There was no way I was losing Jessica or the baby if I had anything to say about it.

But for that, I was prepared for a home birth. I had done all the reading and research. I made certain I had the proper supplies. I would be able to do what I could for the woman I loved and the child she would give us.

Beyond that, we had a small garden, watered by the underground stream that flowed gently from the rock face on the cliff behind our palapa. Perhaps palapa was a misnomer. We'd constructed walls and doors and windows of a sort complete with the trademark thatch roof. It resembled more a swamp chickie common to early Florida natives, minus the stilts.

We were proud of our efforts and results and took much joy in returning to our hacienda every time. The sight of our campsite across the water as we paddled toward it buoyed our spirits immensely. The flagging intensity of dipping paddles in water to get us home was cured by renewed spirits upon sight of the flowers that never failed to greet us.

It served us well, this self-made oasis. It's where Jessica conceived. If she had her way, it would be where our child would be born, too.

We busied ourselves with the day-to-day problems and concerns surrounding our home. We bathed naked together in a catch-basin constructed under the fresh-water spring emanating from the cliff face. Our bank for the gold Jessica discovered stashed in the truck was hidden behind it.

Over time we made friends with some of the Loreto Bay locals. They would boat the short distance down the coast to attend our fish fries. Someone would bring a guitar and we'd sing and dance the afternoon away until it was time to leave.

Jessica's home birth went according to plan, and as it turned out I was involved up to my elbows. I couldn't have been prouder that I helped with the successful birth when I carried mother and daughter Nadja to the truck and hauled them off to the hospital.

The doctor kept us three days. It was only because he wanted to know that mother and baby Nadja were fine before releasing us to return home.

Our tiny nursery was filled with cooing and burping and smiles and laughter, and that was only me. Jessica rolled her eyes at my silliness, and it seemed to me that baby Nadja did, too.

Like mother, like daughter, but that was all right with me. I would have a lifetime with Jessica and Nadja to convince my girls I really was in full possession of my faculties.

Print Books

Jim Nash

Jim Nash The Beginning
Gun Crazy
Gun Crazy 2
Gun Crazy 3
Fallen Angels
Last Stop to Nowhere
Revenge is Justice
Escape / Forget Me Not
Wedding Bell Blues / Breakdown
Mexico Time
LOBO
No Free Ride / Gone
Stealing America
No Escape
Trouble in Paradise

Harry Delaney Adventures

Dead Reckoning
Lie Cheat Steal
Uncharted
Go-Around
Sand Storm
Harry Delaney Adventures

Frank Ross Biker Tales

No Way Out
Bad Girls
Bank Robber Dames

Other

The Last President

About the Author

Peter Duke is a Canadian author. He resides and writes in a small college town in the Province of Ontario.

Aviator. Motorcycle rider. Vagabond. Drifter. Trouble-maker. Jack of all trades and master of none. I've been riding and writing about the places I've been and the people I've seen for a few years now. Some of my writing is factual; some of it isn't. I like to leave it up to readers to decide which lies are the truth.

pxduke.com | peterxduke@gmail.com

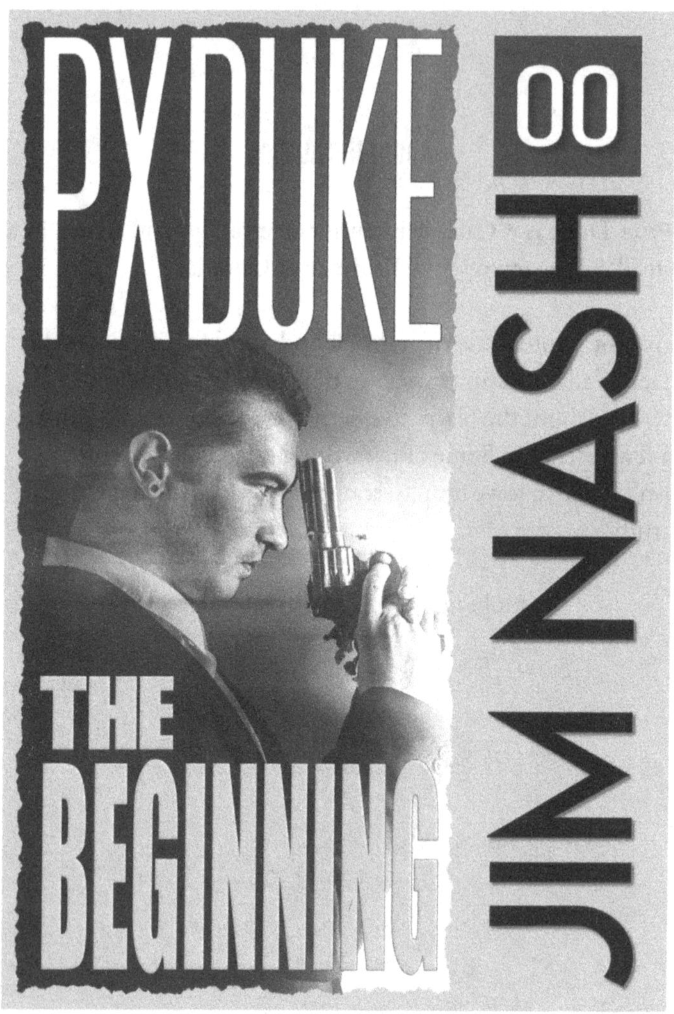

PX DUKE
JIM NASH
00
THE BEGINNING

Jim Nash has to get to Washington, D.C. in a hurry. The plane he chartered is late. There's a private jet sitting on the tarmac in front of him. Buckle up with Nash & Company to find out what the rush is about when Harry Delaney gets hired to fly Jim to a rendezvous neither man will forget.

Check out all six books in the Harry Delaney Adventure series. Find out why Harry makes his way from the North African desert to the Mexican Baja. Discover how he ends up having a triumphal return to the deserts of North Africa.